"Do I Look Like A Mountain Woman?"

Slade stepped into the room and studied Cassie for a minute. "Maybe more like a mountain man's woman," he replied.

The look he gave her, hungry and dark, made her knees turn to liquid.

"I thought I better wash up some myself," Slade said, "or you might wonder what crawled into the cabin during the night."

"I'm already wondering about that." Cassie looked up at the rafters. "Tell me you were kidding about the bats."

"You mean you didn't find any? I guess I've finally managed to bat-proof this place."

Cassie groaned. She knew there'd be no sleep tonight. And she hadn't even *seen* a cot. "Slade, I was wondering, where are we going to sleep?"

He moved around her to the sleeping bag and threw it on the floor. "In my bed, of course."

Dear Reader:

What makes a Silhouette Desire hero? This is a question I often ask myself—it's part of my job to think about these things!—and I *know* it's something you all think about, too. I like my heroes rugged, sexy and sometimes a little infuriating. I love the way our heroes are sometimes just a little bit in the dark about love... *and* about what makes the heroine "tick." It's all part of their irresistible charm.

This March, I want you all to take a good look at our heroes and—if you want—let me know what you think about them!

Naturally, we have a *Man of the Month* who just can't be beat—Dane Lassiter in Diana Palmer's *The Case of the Mesmerizing Boss.* This story is doubly good because not only is it a *Man of the Month* title, it's also the first book in Diana Palmer's new *series,* called MOST WANTED. As for Lassiter, he's a hero you're not likely to ever forget.

Do you think playboys can be tamed? I certainly do! And you can watch one really get his comeuppance in Linda Turner's delightful *Philly and the Playboy.* Barbara McCauley creates a sexy, mountain man (is there any other kind?) in *Man From Cougar Pass,* and Carole Buck brings us a hero who's a bit more citified—but no less intriguing—in *Knight and Day.* And if a seafaring·fellow is the type for you, don't miss Donna Carlisle's *Cast Adrift.*

Some heroes—like some real-life men—are less than perfect, and I have to admit I had a few doubts about Lass Small's *Dominic.* But so many of you wrote in asking for his story that I began to wonder if Dominic shouldn't have equal time to state his case. (You'll remember he gave Tate Lambert such a hard time in *Goldilocks and the Behr.*) Is Dominic a hero? I think he very well might be, but I'm interested in hearing what you all thought about this newly tamed man.

So, I've said all I have to say *except* that I do wish you best wishes for happy reading. Now I'm waiting to hear from you.

Until next month,

Lucia Macro
Senior Editor

BARBARA McCAULEY

MAN FROM COUGAR PASS

SILHOUETTE *Desire*

Published by Silhouette Books New York

America's Publisher of Contemporary Romance

SILHOUETTE BOOKS
300 East 42nd St., New York, N.Y. 10017

MAN FROM COUGAR PASS

Copyright © 1992 by Barbara Joel

All rights reserved. Except for use in any review, the reproduction or utilization of this work in whole or in part in any form by any electronic, mechanical or other means, now known or hereafter invented, including xerography, photocopying and recording, or in any information storage or retrieval system, is forbidden without the permission of the publisher, Silhouette Books, 300 E. 42nd St., New York, N.Y. 10017

ISBN: 0-373-05698-2

First Silhouette Books printing March 1992

All the characters in this book have no existence outside the imagination of the author and have no relation whatsoever to anyone bearing the same name or names. They are not even distantly inspired by any individual known or unknown to the author, and all incidents are pure invention.

® and ™: Trademarks used with authorization. Trademarks indicated with ® are registered in the United States Patent and Trademark Office, the Canada Trade Mark Office and in other countries.

Printed in the U.S.A.

Books by Barbara McCauley

Silhouette Desire

Woman Tamer #621
Man From Cougar Pass #698

BARBARA McCAULEY

was born and raised in California and has spent a good portion of her life exploring the mountains, beaches and deserts so abundant there. The youngest of five children, she grew up in a small house, and her only chance for a moment alone was to sneak into the backyard with a book and quietly hide away.

With two children of her own now, and a busy household, she still finds herself slipping away to enjoy a good novel. A daydreamer and incurable romantic, she says writing has fulfilled her most incredible dream of all—breathing life into the people in her mind and making them real. She has two loud and demanding Amazon parrots, named Fred and Barney, and when she can manage the time, she loves to sink her hands into fresh-turned soil and make things grow.

For Lyn Stimer, who taught me how to climb mountains, and for Barbara Ankrum, who lovingly kicked me up them every step of the way.

One

___

No Trespassing.

Cassandra Phillips slammed on the Jeep's brakes and slid to a stop on the one-lane dirt road. She glared at the large wooden sign. "No trespassing, my eye," she said with disgust. After flying eighteen hundred miles from Boston to Denver, then driving another seventy miles into the most desolate mountain town she'd ever seen, she had no intention of turning back without finding her sister. If I can find this place, Cassie thought dryly, I can certainly find Sarah.

Cougar Pass.

It wasn't even on a map, for God's sake. At least, not the map the car-rental agency had provided. It had taken two gas stations and three attendants before she found someone who'd had actually heard of the town. Although, one general store, one barbershop/tool repair, and one livery/veterinarian, was hardly what

Cassie would call a real town. In all of her twenty-eight years, she'd never seen anything like it.

The people had been friendly, though. When she'd asked three elderly men outside the barbershop if they knew a man named Mason, she'd been given directions by each one of them. Several times. All at the same time.

Shutting off the Jeep's engine, Cassie peered through the dusty windshield and frowned. The sun was dropping much too quickly. She gripped the steering wheel with sweaty palms. It would be getting dark soon, and the thought of wandering around in a pitch-black forest worried her.

This was no time for silly fears of the dark, Cassie chided herself. She stepped out of the car, then grabbed hold of the door to steady herself as dizziness struck. She pressed her forehead to the cool metal. Between the flight, lack of sleep for two days and the altitude, she was light-headed.

Slowly she drew in a deep, pine-scented breath while she waited for her vision to clear. Though the need to hurry pressed in on her, she couldn't resist a moment to take in the magnificence of the forest. Shimmering aspens, tall pines, lush green ferns. Times like this she almost envied her younger sister's free spirit. Cassie couldn't remember the last time she'd had a day out of the office and enjoyed the beauty of a tree. But then, she couldn't remember the last time she'd had a day out of the office at Phillips, Weston and Roe, period.

She closed her eyes and listened. Birds chorused, the wind sang through the taller pines, a gray squirrel chattered angrily close by, obviously objecting to Cassie's intrusion of his territory.

The chilly evening air made her shiver, and she opened her eyes again. Suddenly the immensity of the trees overwhelmed her, the isolation frightened her. The squirrel was right, she thought with a sigh. She didn't belong here.

Cassie reached into the Jeep, grabbed her brown leather jacket and pulled it on over her cable-knit sweater. June weather in the Rockies was much cooler than she'd expected. Shivering again, she grabbed a pair of gloves and a white ski cap. At least she'd had the good sense to wear jeans and comfortable boots, she thought. Practical and level-headed. Isn't that what her father always said about her?

Tugging the cap on, she stuffed the ends of her dark auburn hair under the brim and set off, leaving the car behind. She had no intention of warning Sarah by pulling up to the front door. Whenever her sister wanted to avoid a confrontation, she hid. And Cassie was in no mood to play games. She'd gone too far and was too tired.

That's when she saw the cabin. Dumbfounded, she simply stared. Here, behind a grove of pines, in an honest-to-goodness log cabin, was where her sister had ended up. It was like something out of a wildlife magazine. Smoke billowed out of the rock chimney and an old, pale blue pickup was parked by the front porch. Someone was obviously home. Cassie sucked in a fortifying breath and pulled her cap lower over her ears.

A sneak attack was the best strategy, she decided, moving off the road into the thick trees. She stepped silently over the forest's thick bed of pine needles and maneuvered her way to the side of the cabin, intending to slip around to the front door. Her breath came too quickly, and she gasped in the thin air. She was going to have a few choice words for Sarah this time, Cassie thought. Slinking around corners was not exactly high on her list of fun things to do. Her annoyance quickened her step, and she swung around the front corner of the cabin.

And stared straight down the barrel of a shotgun.

She gasped and the blackness enveloped her.

Of all the things Slade had expected when the intruder stepped around the corner, the most incredible pair of golden-brown eyes was not one of them. He saw her lips part in astonishment as she stared at the gun, then her eyes, those incredible eyes, fluttered shut and she crumpled to the ground.

Moving quickly, he set the gun down and knelt beside her. When he'd noticed the lone figure skulking around in the shadows behind his cabin, he was so amazed he'd simply watched for a few minutes from his kitchen window. Visitors were practically nonexistent up here. His curiosity had quickly turned to anger when he realized that, whoever the person was, he was sneaking around toward the front door.

As if his day hadn't been bad enough, Slade thought wearily. That eagle he'd been tracking for a week had eluded him, and he'd nearly broken his neck when he slipped on a rock and slid twenty feet down a ravine. His backside still ached. All he wanted to do was sit and eat the chicken he was baking and complain to himself in peace.

And now a Peeping Thomasina.

Slade had never dreamed the figure was female. His gaze swept over the still form lying at his feet. Her breathing was shallow, her face pale. Her hair, the color of redwood bark, was partially shoved under a white cap. He pulled the hat off and watched the thick, shiny strands billow around her pale face. He swore silently, feeling a twinge of guilt that he'd scared her.

Why in the hell was a beautiful woman like this sneaking around his cabin?

Since she obviously wasn't answering questions at the moment, Slade effortlessly hefted her over his shoulder. Her body was firm but soft, and when she started to slip from his hold he righted her by placing one hand over her rounded bottom. Nice, he thought. Very nice. He quickly reminded himself the lady was unconscious. And uninvited.

He picked up his gun and set it inside the cabin door, then carried the woman into his living room and kicked the door closed behind him with a boot heel. None too gently, he deposited her on the couch. Her head rolled to one side, and her hair, a tangled mass of mahogany waves, covered her face. He stood over her for a moment, rubbing his chin while he contemplated what to do next. He had no smelling salts. The thought of cold water, however, lifted one corner of his mouth. It would certainly serve the snoop right, he thought. She was lucky he hadn't shot her pretty little head off.

She moaned softly and rolled her head back. Her lashes were thick and dark against her ashen skin. Her neck—long, smooth and enticing—made his throat tighten.

Damn fool woman. Didn't she know how dangerous it could be wandering around in the mountains by herself?

No, she probably didn't, he thought irritably, sitting beside her. He slipped an arm under her and lifted her up as he pulled off her leather jacket. When she fell forward against him, her breasts brushed his chest. His jaw clenched at the contact, and he quickly set her down again. Her soft little moans were remarkably erotic, and his hormones, he realized, were having a sharp jolt out of hibernation.

Forcing his lustful thoughts aside, Slade wondered what in the hell he was going to do with her. She was obviously a city girl, definitely from money. He removed her kid gloves and noted her long, slim fingers. She wore no rings, but he recognized the brand of the gold watch she wore on her slender wrist. Swiss, and very expensive.

She even smelled rich. He indulged himself the simple luxury and breathed in her provocative scent. It was light and spicy. Tempting. The kind of perfume that made a man want to explore soft, heated skin.

And all it would attract up here would be wasps and bees.

It suddenly struck him that perhaps she was a friend of Diane's, but he quickly dismissed the idea. In the two years he'd been married to the woman not one of his ex-wife's rich buddies had come near this place. That, of course, had suited him just fine. They were nothing more than a flock of self-centered phonies, anyway. If he hadn't been so blinded by Diane's pretty face, he would have realized her tenacious pursuit of him had been prompted by boredom, not love. The novelty of marrying a university professor had been irresistible for her—and the biggest mistake she'd ever made, so she'd told him too many times to count.

It had also been the biggest mistake *Slade* had ever made.

A small moan from the intruder brought his attention back to the problem at hand. Who was this woman, and what the hell was she doing here?

He thought briefly about checking her pockets for identification, but as tight as her jeans were, he figured his efforts would merely provide him with a black eye if she woke up. The rise and fall of her breasts beneath the oyster-white sweater she wore was enough to make him swear again.

He grabbed her by the shoulders. "Wake up, lady," he said, giving her a shake. "You've got yourself some explaining to do."

The heavenly aroma of baking chicken filled Cassie's muddled senses. She tried to focus on the wonderful smell and ignore the angry, masculine voice; but whoever he was, he was determined to have her attention. His hands, wrapped around her upper arms, were large and strong. She fought off the heavy fog that veiled her, and slowly opened her eyes.

It was a long heartbeat before she could think, two before she could breathe. Eyes the color of thick smoke glared at her from beneath lowered brows. Her gaze traveled to his lips, which were drawn thin, expressing his impatience. His square jaw was marked with a day's growth of dark beard the same shade of midnight as his wavy hair. He leaned over her, and she could feel the heat of his body, smell pine and damp earth and raw, blatant masculinity. Individually his rugged features never would have been considered handsome, but collectively they were devastating. She stared into his eyes and felt as if she were looking into a mirror, and her own soul—her destiny—was staring back at her.

The feeling panicked her. This was her sister's fiancé, for God's sake. She sat forward too quickly and felt the room spin. Closing her eyes, Cassie leaned back on the sofa and pinched the bridge of her nose between her thumb and forefinger. Her heart was pounding so hard she felt as if she'd just completed a marathon.

That's when she remembered the gun. Her eyes flew open. "You pointed a gun at me!"

He raised one dark brow. "You were sneaking around my house."

He was right about that. Which led her back to the reason she was here. Sighing, Cassie looked around the sparsely decorated room: plaid curtains, brown corduroy couch, one ancient leather armchair. Definitely not Sarah's style. She'd always liked contemporary, glass and chrome. Cassie looked at the man seated beside her. Well-worn jeans, muddy boots, blue cotton work shirt rolled up to his elbows. *He* was not Sarah's style, either. She had always been fascinated by musicians and artists, not muscular lumberjacks.

"Where is she?" Cassie asked pointedly.

"She?"

The ache in her temple began to throb. She'd hoped it wasn't going to be this way, that Sarah wouldn't feel she had to hide. "Mason," she said, trying to hide her irritability, "I've come a long way. I'm tired. You and Sarah don't have to play games with me. Just tell her to come out of hiding and talk with me."

Stunned, he stared at her. What did this crazy woman think? That he had a woman in his closet? The thought almost made him laugh, something he hadn't done in a long time. "Lady," he said, his voice low and assured, "I never play games."

The smooth texture of his voice when he lowered it made Cassie's pulse skip. Dammit anyway, what was the matter with her? It had to be the blasted altitude. She couldn't breathe with this man so close to her.

She jumped up from the couch, but when she moved to take a step, her knees turned to rubber. She started to tumble back, but his hand reached out and caught her elbow. Sparks of electricity shot up her arm.

"You okay?" he asked.

Okay? She was practically swooning because her sister's fiancé touched her. No, she thought, snatching her arm away. She was definitely *not* okay. "Of course I'm all right. I-I'm just a little light-headed."

He pulled himself up beside her, and she lifted her eyes to meet his steely gaze. Good Lord, she thought, he's so *tall*. He had to be at least six foot three.

She drew in a fortifying breath. "Your name's Mason, right?"

He nodded.

"And this is Cougar Pass, right?"

His mouth tightened and he nodded again.

"Well, then—" she pulled a piece of paper out of her pocket "—maybe you can explain this."

She's got to be certifiable, he thought, accepting the letter she handed him. A total nut case. He watched her walk casually backward toward his kitchen, where she glanced over her shoulder. Clenching his teeth, he turned his attention back to the letter. It was addressed to a Cassie Phillips in Boston.

Phillips . . . Phillips . . .

Sarah Phillips.

He stopped reading and looked up at the woman who was inching her way toward the doorway of his bedroom. Rolling his eyes, he opened the letter.

Dear Cassie,
It's always been you who's told me if you have something to say, just say it. So here goes. I've met

a man and I knew instantly he was the one. I know, Cass, I've said that before, but trust me, this time it's real. I've left the Fashion Institute. Mason and I plan to marry as soon as possible. I'm sure you'll understand if I don't tell you where I am. We both know how difficult Daddy can be and how hard it will be for him to accept this. Please know that I'm fine and happier than I've ever been. I promise to call before the wedding. It's important to me that you and Daddy be there.

Forgive me for breaking the news to you this way. Of all the things I don't want to do, it's hurt you. I love you.

Sarah

Now it all made sense, Slade thought, folding the letter. Sarah had mentioned a sister named Cassie. He looked up and watched her peek her head into his bedroom. She actually thought he had a woman in his closet. He shook his head and let out a deep sigh, trying to decide if he should be amused or annoyed. She disappeared into the bedroom, and he frowned.

Annoyed won.

Cassie went into the man's bedroom and glanced around. There was no sign of Sarah anywhere, or any woman for that matter, she noted with surprise. King-size bed, chocolate-brown bedspread. Mismatched dresser and nightstand. No flowers. No feminine touches. Just logs and stone and the barest necessities. She couldn't resist peeking into the already-open wood-paneled closet. Fishing poles, ski jackets, snowshoes. Everything neat and tidy, but no Sarah.

"Would you like to check under the bed, too?"

She whirled at the sound of his voice. He was glaring at her from the doorway, his arms folded stiffly across his broad chest. Sarah's letter dangled from one hand.

"Sorry." She clasped her hands behind her back. "I just got a little carried away." Blushing, she moved away from the closet.

He gave a sarcastic snort of laughter. "Do you really think I stuff women in my closet to hide them from overprotective sisters?"

"I haven't the faintest idea what you do or don't do. Nor do I consider myself overprotective." She stopped in front of him and lifted her chin, forcing herself to ignore the fact that her hands were shaking. His eyes narrowed as he stared down at her. "And if you'll excuse me for saying so," she said, noting the fine but distinct lines around his narrowed eyes, "don't you think you're too, uh, mature for Sarah?"

His jaw twitched. "If you mean I'm too old for her, I hadn't really thought about it."

"Did she tell you she's only eighteen?" Cassie saw the momentary surprise in his eyes. So Sarah hadn't told him. An uneasiness settled high in Cassie's stomach. She sensed this was not the sort of man a woman lied to without serious consequences.

"Look," Cassie hurried on, "marriage is a big decision. One that shouldn't be rushed. You two hardly know each other."

He nodded. "That's true."

Thank God, Cassie thought with relief. At least the man was willing to listen to reason. "Mason," Cassie said gently, "there're some things you don't know about Sarah." He scowled, and she added quickly, "Nothing terrible, of course, but for one, Sarah's not exactly what you might call dependable. This isn't the first time she's done something crazy like this.''

His gaze jerked down to meet hers, and she knew she had his complete attention now. "It's just that . . . well, the past two years have been hard on Sarah since our mother died." She felt the sharp twist in her stomach, but held his gaze, determined not to let him see her own pain. "This year alone I had to bail her out of jail for demonstrating against the building of a nuclear power plant, talk the dean out of expelling her from college three times, and—" she chose her words carefully now "—she hid out at my place twice to avoid a confrontation with an old boyfriend."

His scowl deepened. Cassie swallowed hard. No man wanted to hear about his lover's past relationships. "Honestly," she went on quickly, "I'm not trying to hurt you. In fact, I can see why she fancies herself in love with you. After all, you're very good-looking and I'm sure this mountain-man stuff holds a great deal of appeal for most women—"

"And you're not most women."

She hesitated. "I'd like to think I'm not."

"You've got a point there." He leaned casually against the doorjamb. "I can't remember ever having a woman in my bedroom that I hadn't invited."

His gaze skimmed over her as if she were a book he considered reading, pausing here and there at what might be a "good part." Her heart stopped for a split second then accelerated. She was more than beginning to understand how Sarah could fall for a man who radiated this kind of virility. She knew he was toying with her, though, and that realization made her angry. She took a step back.

"Mason, I don't know what you're up to, unless maybe you're stalling for time so Sarah can avoid having to face me."

"You know," he said, unfolding his arms, "since we're in my bedroom together, alone, I really think we should get the name straight. My name is Slade." He pushed away from the doorjamb. "Slade Mason."

Cassie stared at him, confused. Slade Mason? Sarah's letter had only referred to her new love as "Mason." She'd assumed that was a first name. She took another hesitant step back. Had she gotten the wrong man?

"You—you aren't the Mason in the letter?"

He shook his head slowly and stepped closer.

Though he could have been lying, somehow Cassie knew he wasn't. "But—"

"Mason is my cousin," he explained. "He prefers to go by our last name."

"Oh," she said quietly. "Well, then, I apologize for bothering you. If you'll just give me my letter back and tell me where I can—"

He stepped toward her again, stopping six inches away. "You're not used to making mistakes, are you?"

"Well, not as a rule."

"And you also think you have the right to interfere in other people's lives?"

She stiffened. "Now wait a minute—"

"No, you wait a minute." He grabbed hold of one belt loop on her jeans and pulled her against him. "Nobody, not a sister, not a father, no matter how well-intentioned, has the right to stick their nose where it doesn't belong."

He shoved the letter in the front pocket of Cassie's jeans and let her go. Eyes wide, she stumbled backward. "If you'll excuse me," he said, turning away from her, "I have a chicken that's probably burned by now."

Shaken by the abrupt contact of her body with his, Cassie stood there, her mouth open, and watched him walk out. Three seconds later she was on his heels.

"She's only eighteen, for God's sake," she practically yelled. "Doesn't that mean anything to you?"

He stopped and whirled. She ran straight into the solid wall of his chest. His hands reached out to steady her before she fell. "It means she's of legal age to make her own decisions, last I heard."

"Legal?" Cassie jerked out of his hold. "I'm talking about my sister, and the fact that she's about to make a big mistake."

He folded his arms. "Says who?"

"Says me!" She was too angry to consider he was seven inches taller than her and as unmovable as a concrete column. "I know Sarah, how impulsive she is, how many times she's gotten herself into trouble then come to me to get her out of it."

He thought about that for a moment. "I don't see her coming to you now."

Cassie let out a long breath. "Maybe not this minute, but what about tomorrow, or next week, or next month? What can she possibly know about marriage at her age? What if she rushes into this, then realizes Mason really isn't what she wants?"

"Then it's *her* mistake," he said flatly, "and she'll deal with it. That's how it works in the real world, or didn't you know?" He leaned close. "Tell me, what's really bugging you, Miss Phillips? Is it that you and your father are worried Mason may not fit into your elite circle of Boston society? That maybe he won't know the proper people, or how to dress at one of your fancy affairs? Or maybe—'' he grabbed her hand and held it up ''—that he can't afford gold watches or fancy cars?''

She snatched her hand from his, furious that he was half-right. Her father did feel that way. But not her. Never her. ''I don't have to defend myself to you, Mr. Mason. Just tell me where my sister is and I'll be on my way. I believe we would both find that agreeable.''

A chill shivered up her spine as she met his gaze. His eyes were as cold and hard as granite. He scared the hell out of her, but it had nothing to do with his size, or because she thought he might hurt her. Furious with herself and her lack of composure, she clenched her fists, resisting the urge to take a step back.

From the kitchen, the sound of a sizzling chicken broke the tense silence, and the delicious smell was enough to make her dizzy again. Her stomach growled, and she realized she hadn't eaten since early this morning.

Abruptly he turned away from her and moved into the kitchen where he pulled the chicken out of the oven and set the hot pan on the counter.

''Well?'' She followed. ''Are you going to tell me where Sarah is?''

''No.''

''What?'' She'd been eyeing the chicken so hard she almost missed his answer.

He tossed the hot pads on the counter and faced her. ''Do you have a hard time understanding that word, lady? I said no. N-O. As in no can do. Or perhaps, to put it more succinctly, get lost.'' He took a plate out of the cupboard and set it on the table.

Damn if the man wasn't insufferable! "I understand the word, Mr. Mason," she said carefully. "I simply don't accept it." She decided to try another tactic. "Look, Slade, I'm sorry. I can't possibly expect you to understand about my family. Just do this for me. Call your cousin. Let me talk to Sarah on the phone."

"Can't." He took a knife out of the drawer.

"And why can't you?" she asked through gritted teeth.

"Because Mason doesn't have a phone."

Good grief, it was worse than she'd thought. The man couldn't even afford a phone. God only knew what kind of conditions Sarah was living in. "Okay," she said tightly, struggling for control, "how about this? You could take a message for me, and I'll wait here."

Slade thought about that one for a minute. "That's a possibility."

Cassie drew in a deep breath and smiled. Finally, at least the man wasn't *completely* unreasonable.

"Tomorrow."

"*Tomorrow?* What do you mean, tomorrow? I'm here *now*, tonight."

"Take it or leave it."

He simply stared at her, and she could see from the hard expression on his face he meant exactly what he'd said. She thought about the shotgun she'd noticed lying next to the front door, but discarded the idea. She'd probably just shoot her own foot off.

She turned away, refusing to let him see her tears of frustration. All she'd wanted to do was collect Sarah and go home. And if it wasn't for this man standing in her way, she could do exactly that. She felt a sinking sensation in the pit of her stomach and knew she'd lost this battle.

But not the war.

"You, Slade Mason—" she squared her shoulders "—are the most pigheaded man I've ever met."

She grabbed her jacket and stomped out the front door, well aware of the fact that she'd resorted to name-calling, and even a little bit ashamed of herself for it.

She hesitated on the front steps and tried to put herself in Slade's shoes. If she were sitting quietly at home and he came sneaking around the corner of her house, demanding to know where his cousin was, she'd send him packing, too. Obviously Slade cared for Mason, and he felt she had no business interfering. She could understand that.

Cassie sat down on the porch steps, debating her next move. It was dark, an hour's drive back to town, and she was so tired she couldn't see straight. Swallowing her pride, she stood, then walked back into the house and straight to the kitchen. He was sitting at the table.

"Now do you think we could talk about this like two adults?" she said, crossing her arms.

He grinned up at her and pointed to a chair. He'd set a place for her. "Well," he drawled, "it might not be as much fun, but I'm willing to try if you are."

She stared down at the plate, then looked back up at his smug face. "You knew I'd come back?"

"Lady," he said, laughing, "a woman as determined as you are was bound to come back."

"You're right." She pulled out the chair and sat. "I am determined. And in spite of what you think, I do love my sister and I only want what's best for her."

Frowning, Slade stabbed a chicken breast and dropped it on Cassie's plate.

She put up a hand. "I can't eat your—"

"There's plenty," he interrupted her protest. "I always make extra so I don't have to cook every night."

She was too hungry to argue. She thanked him quietly and picked up a fork.

"So just how do you know what's best for Sarah?" Slade asked, handing her a baked potato.

Cassie knew this line of conversation was only going to lead to another argument. "Mr. Mason—"

"Slade."

"Slade, you've met Sarah, right?"

He nodded.

"And you obviously believe that she and Mason are happy, right?"

As if he suspected she was up to something, he hesitated before he nodded again.

"If they can convince you, I'm sure they'll be able to convince me. Then I can go home and convince my father." She almost choked on those words. That would be the day. *Stubborn* was her father's middle name, in capital letters.

"And what if she can't convince you?" he asked. "What then?"

Cassie shrugged. She could hardly tell him she had no intention of going home without Sarah. "Is there some reason you think I won't approve of Mason?"

His fingers tightened around his fork. "I don't give a damn what you approve of, Miss Phillips. But I'll answer your question, anyway. Mason is a good man. The kind of good that's not measured by the size of a man's bank account, but the size of his heart." He rested his elbows on the table and leaned forward. "Do you know about heart, or is that blue blood of yours pumped through gold-plated veins by sheer egocentricity?"

Egocentric? Blue blood? Cassie struggled to fight back the rage threatening to take over. Of all the judgmental, arrogant— No matter how hungry or exhausted she was, she didn't have to sit here and take this kind of verbal abuse. Not even for Sarah. Her chair scraped the wooden floor as she rose. His hand snaked out across the table and grabbed her wrist.

"I'm sorry," he said quietly. "That was uncalled-for."

"Let go of me."

"If you'll promise to sit back down."

Her voice was low and even. "Let go of me."

He released her. She stood there, rubbing her wrist. Her gaze met his, and she stared at him for a moment, too angry to speak.

He sighed. "Cassie, it seems that each of us has buttons that are better left unpushed. Let's just avoid the subject of Mason and Sarah, at least until after dinner. Then we can put on some boxing gloves and discuss it again."

The thought of an uppercut to Slade's chin made Cassie smile. And it would surely release some of the tension she was feeling toward him. She sat at the table again. "So what shall we talk about, then?"

"Well," Slade said, "I'd be interested in hearing more about how you understood why Sarah was in love with me." He grinned. "Or maybe we could talk about why you think I'm good-looking?"

She almost choked on a bite of chicken. Her cheeks felt as hot as the steaming potato on her plate. "I—well, what I meant was that, uh, that *Sarah* might fall for your type."

"Uh-huh." He chewed thoughtfully. "What type is that?"

Oh, good grief, she was only digging herself in deeper. "Well, the, uh, rugged type. Paul Bunyan, Grizzly Adams, you know. That type."

His lips twitched as he held back a smile. "And you, of course, aren't attracted to that sort of man, are you? Especially me being so old and all. I mean, thirty-four is practically ancient."

"I didn't mean you were too old for me, I meant you were too old for—" She stopped herself. This was getting out of hand. She was beginning to wonder if they wouldn't be better off switching back to the subject of Mason and Sarah. Any conversation would be better than this one.

She decided to avoid his question. "I'm a city girl, Slade. I don't know too much about life outside tall buildings and subways. And even though I do appreciate a tree and an occasional squirrel, this isolation would make me crazy." She reached for the pepper and sprinkled it liberally on her potato. "I can't imagine what you do up here all day long."

At last she found an opportunity to pursue a safer subject. "By the way, what *do* you do? For a living, I mean?"

Slade rose and moved to a small refrigerator beside the stove. "I watch trees grow, mostly," he said, pulling out a carton of milk. He closed the door and returned to the table. "And sometimes, when I'm feeling especially ambitious, I hike around to see what new critters have moved in."

Cassie had no idea what to say without insulting him. He was kidding. He had to be. But from the expression on his face, he was dead serious. Could it really be possible this man did *nothing,* besides watch the flora and fauna, or "critters," as he called them? How could he be in such good shape, she thought, admiring his well-muscled arms and broad chest, if that's all he did? All she could think of to say was, "How interesting."

"Some days it is, some days not," he said, leaning back. Though there was no smile on his lips, Cassie could have sworn she saw one in his eyes. "Now, let me guess what you do." He studied her for a moment. "Sarah told me your father owns an accounting firm, so I would say you probably work for your father."

There was a smug arrogance in his manner that made Cassie bristle. "What are you implying, that nepotism got me my job?" How dare he—a man who did nothing more than watch trees grow—insult her ability to get a job? "I'll have you know I studied my butt off at Stanford for four years to get my degree in business. Nobody handed it to me. I earned it, just like I earned my job."

Slade watched Cassie's cheeks flush red with anger. Her eyes flashed, and the way she tilted her chin upward gave her the look of an indignant cat. But it was her lips that drew his attention at the moment, lips just full enough and wide enough to fit a man's mouth perfectly. He didn't mean to stare, it just happened. And the longer he stared, the redder her face got.

He also realized he'd just pushed one of her buttons. "Touchy, aren't we?" he said, annoyed that just looking at her caused his own heartbeat to pick up. He shook his head. "Your father's accounting firm is highly successful, you're his daughter, why wouldn't you work there?"

Chagrined, Cassie settled back in her chair. "Sorry," she offered with an apologetic smile. "I've had to put up with an occasional comment about my position in my father's company. Maybe I am a little sensitive."

It was amazing how brilliant her eyes shone when she smiled, Slade noted. The color of warm brandy. She had an energy about her, a buoyancy, that radiated from an inner strength. And it was this strength that had sent her looking for her wayward sister. He had a strong feeling that Cassie had no intention of leaving Cougar Pass without Sarah—whether Sarah wanted to go home or not. Slade knew he was going to have to think hard about what to do with Miss Cassie Phillips.

"Just what exactly is your position?" he asked.

"Human Resources—employee relations." She grinned. "I spend most of my time persuading people to see things my way, making people happy, and helping employees at the firm get along with each other."

When Slade raised his brows, Cassie laughed aloud, obviously seeing the incongruity of her statement and her first meeting with him. She rested her forearms on the table and leaned forward. "While I can understand your doubts, I really am good at my job." She sighed and her smile faded. "But I'm afraid when it comes to Sarah, my personal feelings have a tendency to blur my vision a little."

A little? Slade thought. Deciding it best not to say her "blurry vision" was more like a thick blindfold, he simply sat back, considering the situation. What if he'd read the situation wrong between Sarah and Mason? What if there was some truth in what Cassie was telling him, and Sarah's engagement to his cousin was just another escapade of a bored little rich girl? While it definitely went against his grain to interfere in anyone else's business, Slade didn't want to see Mason hurt, either. If Sarah was as flighty as Cassie said, maybe it would be better if Mason found out now, before it was too late.

As it had been for him.

Cassie watched Slade carefully, her breath held. She knew that he was thinking about helping her. She could see it in his face, in the way he was looking at her. She could also see the indecision in his eyes and the lowering of his brows. What she didn't understand was the sudden scowl, the cold, fierce expression that crossed his rugged features. He was going to say no. She knew it. She let her breath out slowly, readying herself to do battle.

"Okay, Cassie," he said, startling her. He stared at her with intense, dark eyes. "You want to talk to Sarah and meet Mason, I can arrange it."

She felt a river of relief run through her. She had no idea what made him change his mind, but she wasn't about to question her good fortune. "Thank you" was all she could manage.

"Tomorrow."

"But—"

He leaned forward, the scowl pronounced, his voice as hard as his eyes. "I said, tomorrow. Don't make me regret it, or I can easily be convinced to change my mind."

She clamped her mouth shut, gritting her teeth. All right, let him have it his way. One more day couldn't matter all that much. And besides, she was tired. Exhausted, was more the word. She nodded. "You're the boss." For the moment. She rose and began clearing the table. "What time shall I come back in the morning?"

He took the dishes from her and set them on the sink counter, then turned on the water. "You don't have to come back."

"Excuse me?"

"I said—" he poured soap into the sink "—you don't have to come back. You can stay here."

Two

For a moment she thought maybe she hadn't heard him right. He was suggesting she stay *here?* Ridiculous. "I, uh, hardly think that would be a good idea."

"Why?" He took the dish she offered and ran it through the sudsy water.

"Well, because...because..." She was stammering, dammit. It wasn't as if she was a child, for heaven's sake. She cleared her throat. "Because I don't know you, that's why."

He pulled his arms out of the water, and bubbles covered his forearms. Gripping the edge of the sink, he turned. "I didn't ask you to sleep in my bed, Cassie, I simply said you could sleep here—" he pointed to the living room "—on my couch." He smiled widely, his teeth white and even. Amusement lighted his eyes. "If I was offering anything more than the couch, I'd come right out and say it."

The blatant sexual overtones of his words made her heart pick up its pace. She felt her cheeks grow warm, and cursed herself for acting like such a schoolgirl. Generally she wasn't nervous around men. But then she'd never been around a man like Slade. He was brash, outspoken, too damn sure of himself. She didn't quite know how to deal with a man like him. Or if she *could* deal with him. She had learned there were men, like her father, who could only be dealt with on their own terms. The best you could hope for was to come out of a situation with some kind of compromise—a compromise that *they* suggested.

But stay here? She glanced around the cabin and suddenly felt as if she were in a matchbox. It was completely dark outside now, town was an hour's drive away, and she knew she was too tired to make it safely back down the narrow mountain road. It was neither practical nor expedient to leave.

She drew in a deep breath and turned to meet his gaze. There was an unspoken dare in his smoky eyes. Straightening her shoulders, she reached for a dirty pan and handed it to him.

"The couch will be fine, thank you."

Absolute quiet was the thing that finally woke Cassie early the next morning. At her apartment in Boston it would have been a garbage truck rumbling down the street, or the man next door who loved to sing in the shower, or that little Pekingese across the hall barking every morning as Mrs. Fraser took it for a walk. Here, six thousand feet up, it was *too* quiet. She needed some noise. A radio. A television. Anything to break this deadly silence.

Pushing herself up on her elbows, she rolled her head to loosen the knots in her neck. Sleeping on Slade's couch had not exactly been what she'd call comfortable. She sat up and swung her bare feet onto the cold hardwood floor, then reached for her overnight bag beside the couch.

After dinner last night Slade had offered to retrieve the Jeep for her. Since the thought of wandering around the forest in the pitch black had terrified her, she'd eagerly accepted. He'd actually seemed relieved to get out of the cabin. Based on the irritable mood he was in, she imagined he was used to being alone, and having another person around probably made him tense. No matter, she thought, pushing the blanket aside. She'd be gone today and life could get back to normal for both of them.

As she tiptoed through the living room she glanced over at the closed bedroom door, then at her watch. It was past seven. Considering how early he'd gone to bed last night, she assumed he'd be up by now. She always thought that people who lived in the mountains woke up at four o'clock every day, then went out to chop wood or some mountainy thing like that. She sighed. Hadn't she learned it was best not to assume with a man like Slade?

Quietly she stepped into the bathroom and closed the door. Maybe Slade was just plain lazy. Since he obviously had no real job, perhaps he slept a lot, or went fishing every day. Somehow, though, she kept rejecting that idea. She had a feeling there was more to the man than he was telling her.

She showered in record time, then quickly slipped on her jeans and a clean yellow T-shirt. When she stepped out of the bathroom again the bedroom door was still closed. She frowned. Was he going to sleep all day? She wanted to get this business over with and be on a plane back to Boston. With Sarah. Lightly she knocked on the door.

"Slade," she whispered sweetly. "You awake?"

No answer. She knocked again. Louder.

"Slade?"

Still no answer. Good grief, was the man hibernating? She chewed on her bottom lip, worrying what a person does when they wake up a sleeping bear. Run like hell? She glanced down at her bare feet. She hoped not. She opened the bedroom door and peeked in. His bed was made. Neat as a pin.

He was gone!

Cassie raced back to the living room and looked out the front window. The Jeep was still parked there, as was his truck. She ran to the kitchen and glanced out the back window. Not a sign of him.

She muttered a curse under her breath. Maybe he'd pulled a fast one on her and had already taken off to warn Sarah. The sneak! To think that she'd trusted him, believed that he would take her—

That's when she saw him. Dressed in a red-and-black plaid shirt and black windbreaker, he came out of a shed on the edge of his property where the woods started. Relieved, she started to chastise herself for thinking such unkind thoughts about him, until she saw him turn and head into the woods.

Loaded down with . . . a backpack?

If he was going to warn Mason and Sarah, why would he need a full backpack? Why wouldn't he simply take the truck? Maybe he'd changed his mind about letting her talk to Sarah, or maybe he'd lied. What if he was going off into the woods and leaving her alone until she gave up and went home? Anger surged through her. She'd be damned if she'd let him make a fool out of her that way!

She had her socks and boots on in two blinks, pulled on her sweater, then grabbed her jacket and ran out the back door, following the same path Slade had taken. When she caught up with him, she thought, she'd give him a piece of her mind.

The air had a chilling bite to it, and Cassie stopped to put her jacket on. She listened for some kind of a sound that might tell her which way Slade had gone. Wind rushed through the tall pines like the distant roar of a waterfall. Birds chattered overhead while they hunted for breakfast, and one big blue jay stared at her from the lower branch of a small fir. Cassie hadn't a clue which direction to take.

"So which way did he go?" she asked the bird, who let out a caw, then was gone.

The scent of damp wood and pine filled the woods. Through the tops of the trees she could see the sky was already a pristine blue, with a white penciling of clouds on the distant horizon. Any other day she might have taken the time to enjoy the beauty around her. But not now. Not today.

Cassie knelt down and studied the ground where she'd seen Slade disappear. Boot prints in the soft dirt veered off to the left.

"Okay, Mr. Mountain Man," she said out loud, "you aren't going to get away so easily." She smiled to herself, thinking how surprised he'd be when she showed up. She couldn't wait to see the look on his face.

Forty-five minutes later she was hopelessly lost.

Every tree looked the same. Every rock. Every pine needle, every twig. She was in the middle of a clearing now, no longer on a path, and she hadn't seen or heard the slightest sound that might be Slade. She was definitely in trouble.

Panic gripped her. She hadn't the faintest idea which way to go. There were no street signs, no pedestrians to ask directions. She was completely out of her element.

Stay calm, she told herself, then sat down on a large, overturned tree trunk to consider her options. She couldn't risk heading farther into the woods. She might never find her way out. Though Cassie hated to admit it, she knew she should go back to the cabin and wait Slade out. While that thought didn't appeal to her, it was better than starving to death in the woods, or falling off a cliff and ending up at the bottom of some ravine. Besides, at least there would be *some* satisfaction in letting the man know she wasn't going to give up and go home without talking to her sister.

She'd have to go back. There was only one problem.

Which way was back?

She stood and brushed her hands off on the seat of her jeans. It would be easy, she'd just follow her own footsteps back and—

The sound of twigs snapping and leaves rustling brought her up short. So he *had* come back, she thought with a smug grin. He'd probably realized she was following him and was trying to sneak up on her just to rattle her. She turned, prepared to let him know just exactly what she thought of his devious tactics.

Only it wasn't Slade.

About fifty feet from her, at the edge of the clearing, was the biggest, blackest bear Cassie had ever seen. Its huge snout sniffed at the air. She felt as if her heart had leapt up into her throat, cutting off all sound.

"Stay calm, stay calm," she repeated over and over.

Never taking her eyes off the creature, she backed up slowly.

"S-Slade," she whispered, her voice cracking. The bear rose on his hind legs and watched her retreat with interest, but made no move to come after her.

"Slade," she said louder this time, praying he was within earshot. When the creature dropped back down on all fours, Cassie screamed.

"Slade!"

She whirled, prepared to fly if necessary, and ran smack-dab into the solid chest of a man. The force of the contact sent her sprawling backward and she landed with a loud *whoof* on her backside.

"Good God, Cassie, what are you doing?" Slade stood over her, rubbing his chest, his face set in a frown.

"Bah-bah—" She pointed frantically behind her.

"What?"

Still pointing, she scrambled up and ran behind him. She almost sighed in relief as she noticed the gun in his hand.

"Spit it out, woman, I can't stand around here all day."

"B-bear!" she finally managed, grabbing his arm. "Over t-there." She buried her face into his back and clung to him, waving a finger in the direction she'd just come from.

He looked away, then back again. "What bear?"

"Over there," she shouted, fighting down her panic. "Right there! Shoot it!" Lifting her head, she pointed again and peered over his shoulder.

It was gone.

Slade glanced over at her. She could see the doubt in his eyes.

"It was there, I tell you! Right over there!"

"Well," he drawled, "it's not there now. All your hollering probably scared it away."

"*I* scared *it?*" Still shaking, she hung on to Slade, not quite ready to let go. The strength she felt in his muscled arms reassured her. "You're kidding, right? I was almost lunch for some ferocious animal, and you're making jokes." She clung to him. "You're a sick man, Slade."

Slade pried Cassie loose and pulled her around to face him. "Unless it was a female with cubs, you really wouldn't be in any danger. Bears aren't used to humans around here. If you actually did see one—"

"What do you mean, *if?*" She jerked away from him. "What are you saying? That I'm making it up?"

He shrugged. "Well, when you're lost, your imagination can get carried away and—"

"And just how did you know I was lost?" She crossed her arms and raised her chin, meeting his amused expression with her own heated gaze. "Unless, of course, you've been following me."

"Actually," he said, slipping the backpack off his shoulders, "*you* were the one following me. Only you sort of lost your way, didn't you, Little Miss Riding Hood?" He gave her a wide smile and pointed behind her. "Grandma's house is *that* way."

She looked where he pointed. Good grief, she never would have thought that was the way to the cabin. "I knew that."

"Really?" He raised one eyebrow.

"Of course."

"Then you can just go back." He slipped the gun into his backpack. "By yourself."

By herself? She swallowed hard and glanced around the woods. Before the bear, they'd seemed beautiful, peaceful. Now...

"I have no intention of going back." She squared her shoulders. "Since you've obviously welshed on our agreement, I'm not going to let you out of my sight."

His eyes narrowed. "Just what do you mean, 'welshed on our agreement'?"

She pointed to the backpack. "The way I see it, Mr. Mason, you were taking off on a little vacation in the woods, leaving me high and dry."

"Oh, that's the way you see it, huh?"

She nodded. "You probably figured I'd give up and go home."

"I was hoping, that I'll admit." One side of his mouth twitched upward.

"Well, I'm not going home." She leaned forward. "You promised to take me to Sarah, and—"

"Hold on, there." The amusement she'd seen in his eyes a moment before was gone now. "I said I'd arrange for you to talk to her, not that I'd take you to her. Sarah is your problem, not mine."

"Problem?" Cassie ground her back teeth together. "I hardly consider Sarah a problem, Slade. She's my sister. I'm worried about her. Why can't you understand that?"

"I understand perfectly," he said curtly. "You're the one who seems to have forgotten that Mason is my cousin, more like a brother, considering he lived with my family from the time his parents were killed when he was eight."

Anger drained away, replaced by a weary sadness. Cassie closed her eyes, drawing in a slow breath. She'd been twenty-six when her mother died unexpectedly, and she'd nearly fallen apart. How could a little boy survive that kind of trauma? "I—I'm sorry. I didn't know."

She and Slade were both trying to protect the people they loved. She couldn't fault him for that. He was doing exactly what she would do if the situation was reversed.

"You're right." She opened her eyes again and saw the surprise on his face. "Really, I mean it. I appreciate all you've done for me, especially considering the way I've barged in here. Dinner last night, the couch." She smiled at him, rubbing the small of her back. "Though I'm not so sure about the couch."

With a sigh, she looked up at the tops of the trees. "I'm afraid living in the city all my life has made me cynical, Slade. It's hard to know who to trust anymore." She lowered her eyes and met his steady gaze. "I don't know how else to make you understand how important Sarah is to me. I need to know she's all right, that she's happy. I love her. How can I just walk away?"

For what seemed like an eternity, Slade stared at her. She could see the uncertainty in his eyes.

"Sometimes," he said softly, "when you love someone, the best thing for them is to let them go."

He stepped closer and plucked pine needles from her tangled hair. Shivers raced up her spine, startling her. She had the most incredible, insane urge to turn her cheek into his hand. The forest wrapped around them like a protective cocoon and she was lost again, this time in the charcoal depths of Slade's eyes. The look frightened her, perhaps more than the bear. She pulled away.

"I'll think about that." Her legs shaking, she walked away. "Back at the cabin."

"Cassie."

She stopped.

"It's a long hike to Mason's cabin."

Was he saying what she thought he was saying? Her heart racing, she turned. "I've got boots on."

He smiled. "No, I mean it's a *long* hike."

"How long is long?"

His gaze was steady. "Two days."

"Two days!" He had to be kidding. Nobody could live in that kind of isolation. Certainly not Sarah. "You're telling me in order to get to Mason's house, we have to walk through the woods?"

"It's the most direct route from here."

"Two days is direct?" she gasped.

"Maybe a little less," he said, "if there're no problems."

She closed her eyes, afraid to ask. "What kind of problems?"

He shrugged. "Weather, what kind of shape you're in."

She straightened. "I'm in great shape, but this is ridiculous, I can't go off like this, with you, into the wilderness for two days."

"You're right," he said, hoisting the backpack higher, "it was just a thought." He turned and started to walk away. "Just sit tight and I'll be—"

"Wait."

He stopped and glanced over his shoulder at her. She swallowed hard. "I . . . don't have a sleeping bag . . . or clothes, or anything. Maybe we could go back and get my things."

Slade shook his head. "We're too far away to go back and head out again. I have a rest camp a day's walk from here, and we can make it before dark if we leave now. Most everything you need I have there." He grinned. "What I don't have extra, we can share."

That thought of sharing with Slade brought about the most unusual twinges in her stomach. She hesitated, considering what she was getting herself into. Alone, in the woods, with this man for two days?

"It was a bad idea." He reached in his shirt pocket and pulled out a compass. "Just follow this northeast and you'll end up back at the cabin in about an hour."

It was a challenge, pure and simple, Cassie thought. He didn't think she could handle it. But Slade Mason didn't know the stuff Cassandra Phillips was made of, she thought, setting her jaw.

Her decision made, she moved toward him and stopped a few inches away. She pulled the compass from his hand and shoved it back into his pocket. "It won't be necessary." She raised her eyes to meet his dubious gaze. "I'm coming with you."

"I don't think—"

"I'm going, Slade. You asked me and I won't let you take it back. So let's stop arguing and get about it." She pushed ahead of him and walked briskly away.

"Cassie."

She turned. He was grinning wider than a Cheshire cat. "You're going the wrong way."

Two hours later, beside a wide, rushing stream, Slade decided that Cassie needed a rest. Not that she would have ever admitted it, he thought with a smile, though for the last two miles she'd slowly dropped farther and farther behind him. He'd been in back of her for a while, but it was far easier on his nerves for him to lead, he decided. He had a difficult time keeping his mind on anything other than her rounded bottom in tight jeans.

It was a distraction he didn't need or want right now. He set his backpack down on the grass-covered bank of the stream and hunkered down, waiting for her to catch up.

She'd surprised him. With her fancy leather boots and gold watch, she was obviously a city girl to the core. Yet she hadn't complained once, not even when they'd had to climb about fifty feet through that rocky ravine. There appeared to be more than one dimension to Cassie Phillips. He found that thought intriguing.

He watched her emerge from the dense woods and approach, her long hair a wild mass of mahogany curls around her flushed face, her lips parted as she breathed heavily. She looked like some kind of exotic forest creature, wild and untamed. She'd removed her jacket and sweater about an hour ago as the day had warmed, and the yellow T-shirt she wore underneath—damp now from perspiration—hugged the fullness of her breasts. Not liking the direction his mind was taking, or the response his body was having, he forced himself to look away from her. He was on a mercy mission here. Nothing else.

When he looked back he saw her at the edge of the clearing, fists at her waist, scanning the area in search of him. He almost laughed out loud. Here he was, no more than sixty feet away, and she'd managed to get herself lost again.

When she'd gotten herself lost earlier this morning, he *had* been following her. Once he'd heard her behind him in the woods, his curiosity had gotten the better of him. He'd backtracked around behind her and kept an eye on her, watching from a distance.

He smiled again. He didn't think he'd tell her that he *had* seen the bear, also. Let her wonder about that.

"Over here." He raised a hand. Her face lighted up as she saw him. Smiling, she hurried forward, and the excitement he saw in her face widened his own smile. It had been a long time since a woman had looked at him like that. He liked the warm feeling it gave him. Of course, he realized abruptly, she wasn't actually looking at him like *that,* she was simply glad he wasn't a bear.

Cassie forgot all about her aching feet the second she saw Slade sitting beside the stream. She'd lost sight of him for a few minutes and she'd started worrying she might be lost again. He never would have let her live *that* down. Of course, if she'd been lost, she might not have lived at all, considering her abilities as an outdoor woman. Not to mention bears and snakes and God knows what. She hesitated for a moment. She hadn't considered snakes before. She hated snakes.

"What's the matter?" Slade asked as she came up beside him. A worried frown had replaced the smile.

She poked around through the thick grass with the toe of her boot. "Well, nothing, exactly," she said, circling a large, moss-covered rock a foot away. "It's just that, uh, I was wondering, how many snakes are there around here?" She kicked at a large piece of bark and turned it over.

"Not many." He patted the cool grass next to him. "Sit down and don't think about it. I'll let you know when to worry."

Still unsure, Cassie started to sit, then glanced over at the stream. Her throat felt like cotton. "Can we drink that water?"

"What?"

"The water." She gestured toward the stream. "You know, is it clean?"

Finally understanding, he laughed. "There are a few places left where the water's still good, Cassie. Unless, of course, you only drink the stuff that comes out of a bottle with a fancy name." He walked to the edge of the stream, scooped out a handful and drank it.

She moved up next to him as he reached down again. "It's also terrific for cooling down." Using both hands, he scooped up more water and threw it at her, catching her in the face.

Cassie gasped, too stunned to move for a moment. Water dripped off her nose and the ends of her hair. She glanced down, then slowly raised her head.

Slade saw the look of retaliation in her amber eyes. She pressed her lips together and took a step toward him. He backed away, laughing.

"Is that what you call mountain-man humor?" She sidestepped his retreat and he moved back toward the bank.

"More like fifth grade," he choked out, still grinning. "You did ask how the water is, you know."

It surprised Cassie that Slade had a sense of humor, if one would call splashing water a sense of humor. Whatever it was, it wasn't something she could let pass.

She threw up her arms and let out a sigh. "Would you just look at this?" She glanced down and pointed to the front of her soaking T-shirt.

Slade's laughter quickly died away as he stared at Cassie. Her breasts were clearly defined beneath her wet shirt, her nipples beaded. He felt his own body grow taut, cursed himself that he couldn't seem to drag his eyes away from the arousing sight of her.

That was when she took advantage of the situation and ran at him.

Three

Surprise registered on Slade's face at Cassie's sudden charge. What she intended to do was slip around him and splash him with a liberal dose of water, but when he dodged her, his foot caught on a loose rock. He stumbled, grabbing hold of her arm as he fell backward into the stream. She felt herself falling with him and let out a shriek. Arms flailing, they both went in, Slade on his rear, Cassie on top of him.

Cold water swirled over them. She gasped, stunned by the chill and the intimate arrangement of her body on top of his.

"Slade!" She tried to pull away from him. "Let me go!"

"What's the matter," he said, grinning up at her, "too cold for you?"

"It's freezing!" She struggled to free herself, then instantly realized her mistake. With their bodies joined so snugly together, her squirming only succeeded in creating a more sensual type of contact. Every inch of him was solid muscle, she noted with a feeling somewhere between admiration and alarm. His hands circled her upper arms, holding her firmly against him. She stilled, but her heart pounded so wildly she knew he could feel it. Her breasts pressed against the hard-rock wall of his chest, and their lower bodies merged as familiarly as lovers. Heat, unexpected and swift, flooded through her, chasing away the cold.

She twisted away from him and stood, staggering back as the water sucked at her ankles. Her wet clothes clung to her like a second skin. Slade's gaze, slow and hungry, moved over her, and she knew she was not the only one who'd been affected by the contact. Awareness sparked between them. Their eyes met, and in that split second either one could have reached for the other and the rest of the world be damned. It was the most basic need between a man and a woman, but Cassie had never felt it so strongly.

She took a step forward, then stopped abruptly. What could she possibly be thinking? These were dangerous feelings with a man like Slade. He was the kind of man that made a woman lose control, forget about priorities and goals. Something she could not afford to do.

Heart still pounding, she turned away and moved to the edge of the bank, telling herself her legs were shaking from the cold.

Slade allowed himself a few extra moments in the stream. The icy current swirled around him and he welcomed it, needing to douse the fire raging in his blood right now. Cassie's lithe, curved body on top of him left him feeling raw with need, aching to pull her against him again.

He didn't like the feeling one damn bit.

Sufficiently cooled down, Slade rose and moved to the bank where Cassie was shaking her arms.

"Darn," she said, glancing at her wrist. "My watch got wet."

Her complaint sharply reminded Slade of the differences in their life-styles. He didn't even own a watch, let alone one that cost more than his pickup.

Dripping, he moved toward her, his face set in a scowl. "I ought to let you find your own way to your sister." He shook his head, and water flew in shining droplets.

She laughed nervously and sat at the edge of the stream. "You started it."

He rolled his eyes. "That's a woman's reasoning for you." He stopped two feet away, then reached for the top button of his drenched shirt.

"More like fifth-grade reasoning, I'd say." She watched him unbutton his shirt and tug it free from his jeans. Her breath held when he pulled it off his shoulders.

Even with her fingers splayed, she realized, her hands wouldn't nearly cover the width of his broad chest. Dark hair liberally dusted his upper torso. As he turned away from her and spread his shirt out on a rock, his muscles flexed and bunched with the same rhythmic strength as the rushing stream. She'd thought him lazy before, but she now knew he couldn't possibly be idle. Strength like his came from plain hard work. But what work? she wondered, watching him. Her pulse grew erratic, and she quickly glanced away, afraid he might turn and see her staring at him with such blatant admiration.

"It'll dry faster if you take it off."

When she turned back, he was grinning at her, his thumbs hooked in the loops of his waistband. The wet hair on his chest glistened, and she couldn't stop her gaze from following the dark triangle that lead to the top snap of his jeans. Her stomach did a flip. "I don't think so."

He shrugged. "Can't blame a guy for trying." He dug into his backpack, then sat beside her. "Lunch." He held out a piece of beef jerky and a package of trail mix.

"I don't suppose you have a hamburger in there?" she asked. When he shook his head, she sighed and accepted the jerky and nuts. She was starving right now, and even a piece of dried-up meat and hamster food was appetizing.

Slade sat beside her, resting his arms on his knees as he ate. Cassie, still embarrassed from their intimate dip in the stream, avoided eye contact with him. She looked at everything around her instead: the glimmering leaves of the aspens, the silvery rush of water over rocks, a lizard sunning itself beside the stream. What she wouldn't give right now to strip off her wet clothing and stretch out on a warm rock.

Slade watched the pensive smile that spread slowly over Cassie's lips. Curious what had brought the smile about, he followed the direction of her gaze and spotted the lizard. Slade was surprised. Considering how she felt about reptiles, he would have expected a frown or grimace. She was a real enigma. On the surface, she was cool and sophisticated, in control. He pictured her in her everyday life: tailored suit, her hair pulled up, her back stiff as she sat behind a big glass desk in a stuffy office.

Now, here she was, on a trek through the wilderness, determined to save Sarah from making what she thought was a disastrous mistake. Was Cassie really worried about saving her sister, or was she, like her father, just concerned that the Phillips's name would be sullied if Sarah married Mason, a man without a penthouse or corner office?

He frowned, then bit down hard into his jerky as he watched her. Sunlight sparkled like drops of fire in her tousled hair, and she stretched her long legs out in front of her, one ankle casually crossed over the other. A few minutes ago in the stream, an image of those legs, wrapped around him, had flashed through his mind. The image reappeared now in erotic detail, and when she licked her lips to catch a sunflower seed, he felt as if a fist were twisting in his stomach.

Damn!

He looked away from her. If he was going to be around her, he damn well better learn to control his overactive libido.

Because he didn't trust himself to look at her, or to speak, he turned his attention to a hawk circling overhead, listening to its cry of greeting when its mate appeared. After a few moments, they swept gracefully out of sight.

His emotions under control again, Slade leaned back and rested his head on his arm as he studied Cassie. She'd closed her eyes and lifted her face to the light breeze ruffling the ends of her hair. "You and Sarah don't look anything alike."

Her eyes opened and she glanced up at him, her gaze questioning.

"Mason brought her over one day shortly after they got here," he explained. "Told me he couldn't wait to show her off."

Cassie's face lighted with pleasure. "Sarah was lucky enough to inherit our mother's blond hair and blue eyes. I, unfortunately, inherited my father's dark looks." She smiled. "I was always envious of Sarah's fairness."

Slade stared at her, slowly chewing his jerky. "You're a beautiful woman, too, Cassie. I can't imagine you being envious of anyone."

Cassie's gaze swept downward, and Slade was amazed when her cheeks flushed pink. He found this demure and unaffected side of her as attractive as the spitfire nature he'd already encountered. Drops of water trickled down her slender neck, and he watched them disappear into the wet neckline of her T-shirt. He couldn't stop himself as his gaze dropped lower. Her breasts, distinctly outlined beneath her damp shirt, made his palms ache. He curled his fingers into fists and quickly looked away.

He was more than questioning his sanity at bringing her along with him. His intention had been to ruffle her feathers a little, crack her smooth composure, but so far he'd only succeeded in aggravating himself. That thought aggravated him all the more.

"You know, Cassie," he said, turning the conversation to the one topic he knew would unnerve her, "the Sarah I met seemed like a mature young woman."

"Really?" she replied coolly, straightening. "And I suppose all *mature,* eighteen-year-old young women leave school to run off with a man they've just met."

He almost smiled at the way her eyes blazed. Like sunlit honey. "There's no accounting for the crazy things people do when they fall in love, is there?"

"I really wouldn't know," she said, brushing her hair back out of her face. "I haven't had a lot of personal experience in that." Brows raised, she met his gaze. "Have you?"

Slade flinched inwardly. He did, but he certainly had no intention of discussing his past, and disastrous marriage, with anyone. Frowning, he sat up. "I'm just saying she doesn't strike me as being as impetuous as you think. Before you go riding in on a white horse, have you considered giving them a chance?"

Her chin lifted. "It's obvious that you and I are never going to be able to discuss Sarah and Mason without getting into an argument. Therefore, since we're stuck together for the time being, I suggest we both steer clear of the subject."

Stuck together? He gritted his teeth. "Fine."

"Good."

"Okay."

Slade stood, resisting the urge to throw Cassie back into the stream. What was the sense in talking to the woman? He'd tagged a marmot last week that had been more willing to listen to reason. He reached for his shirt and yanked it on, then stuffed the wet ends into his jeans and slipped his backpack over his shoulders.

He glanced over at Cassie, standing stiffly with her back to him, arms folded. Her hair, still damp, hung halfway down her back in a wild mass of curls. His gaze swept down over her small waist, rounded bottom, and lingered on her long, long legs. His anger intensified his sudden arousal, and he marched past her without a word. He didn't give a damn who or what Cassie was, he told himself. She'd be gone soon enough, and he wouldn't give her a second thought.

There was only one word for the tiny structure Cassie stood gaping at: barbaric.

Set into the side of a steep ridge, the rough-hewn logs looked like oversize matchsticks stuffed with mud and dried grass. A high-pitched tin roof sat atop the hut like a silly hat, and a window—barely large enough to see into or out of—trimmed the outside edge of the timber-built door.

Slade had told her he kept a small cabin, but this was ridiculous. This place gave new dimension to the word *rustic*.

She approached the hut carefully, as if it were a living thing, keeping her distance in case it decided to bite. Slade, grinning like the proud owner of a luxury home, stopped short of the cabin and folded his arms as he turned to Cassie.

"So, what do you think?"

He wanted her to answer that? "Well, it's, uh, really something."

He laughed. "I thought that's what you'd think."

She followed him to the entrance. "You actually stay in here?" She took a step back when he pulled a rope handle and shoved on the door with his shoulder. Dirt and gravel cascaded from the roof onto his head.

Brushing a hand over his hair, he opened the door wide and looked inside. "Only when I feel the need to get away."

"Get away!" She gave a snort of laughter. "You live a million miles from civilization and you need to get away?"

"Even up here a person can get caught in the 'same time, same place' routine." He coughed and stepped back outside. "Better let it air out," he said, removing his backpack.

"Good idea," Cassie mumbled, thankful for a reprieve from entering what looked to her like a gigantic bird's nest.

The beauty of the forest more than made up for the hut's primitive conditions. No more than twenty feet away, a small waterfall tumbled down a sharp incline and funneled into a shallow pool. Giant cedars, interspersed with smaller conifers, swallowed the surrounding area, scenting the air, as well as providing a lacy umbrella of protection from the warm, late-afternoon sun. A lush undergrowth of ferns dotted the ground, and a brilliant green cloverlike plant enveloped the soft moist soil around the trees' trunks. Her feet aching, she eased herself down and sat on a moss-covered rock.

One thing to be said for a long hike, she noted dryly, was that it had definitely assuaged her annoyance with Slade. Let him think whatever he wanted about her. Why should she care, as long as he took her to Sarah? Besides, she thought as she rubbed one sore calf, she was too tired to be angry anymore.

A small groan caught her attention, and she watched Slade stretch his arms over his head. She couldn't help but admire the narrow tapering of his waist and the muscular expanse of his long legs. His jeans and shirt were dusty, his dark hair peppered with twigs and pebbles. He blended in with these surroundings, wild and undisciplined. She tried, for some strange reason, to imagine him in a three-piece suit. She couldn't.

"Tired?" he asked, walking toward where she sat.

Though her pride would have her lie, she was too exhausted. "Does a forest have trees?" She gestured around her.

He grinned. "That bad, huh?"

"Mister, if that bear shows up for dinner, then I'm it, because I couldn't budge an inch from this rock if my life depended on it."

He knelt down in front of her. "I have an old, mountain-man cure for that."

"Please don't tell me I have to wear the skin of a lizard or drink boiled tree bark."

"Nope." She gasped as he snatched up her right leg and propped it on his thigh. "It's called a good old-fashioned rubdown."

His hands were already working on her sore calf before she could protest, and even through the rough denim of her jeans, his touch was bliss. "Slade, don't," she said, but it was more a groan of delight than a complaint. His fingers kneaded her tender muscles, sending waves of intense pleasure through her. She couldn't have made him stop any more than she could have prevented the sun from rising. His hands worked their magic on her, and she fell under the spell. Closing her eyes, she rolled her head back and sighed.

"You could do this for a living," she said after a moment.

He laughed. "If all my clients looked like you, I just might consider it."

He'd make a fortune, Cassie thought, imagining Slade as a professional masseur. She looked at him through slitted eyes, watching his large, strong hands gently move over her leg. The play of corded muscle on his bared forearms fascinated her. She gripped the sides of the rock she sat on to stop herself from floating away. When he moved to her other leg she groaned softly and let her eyes drift shut. His hands on her were heaven and torture all at the same time.

Slade watched Cassie's head roll back and his throat went dry. He'd simply wanted to ease her discomfort when he'd offered to rub her leg, but now he was having a difficult time sticking to that goal. His body hurt and his fingers ached to feel her skin. It was all he could do not to peel those jeans off her and pull her beneath him. When she groaned again in that husky voice, he thought he might lose it completely.

"Cassie."

From her fog of pleasure, Cassie heard her name being called. It was a desperate sound, almost a plea. "Hmm?" was all she could muster.

"Cassie, if you don't stop looking so damned sexy, I'm not going to be responsible for my actions."

It took a moment for his words to register. She opened her eyes and saw him staring at her with an expression close to pain. She suddenly realized how she must look to him. With her eyes closed and her back arched, she was practically inviting him to make love to her. His fingers moved up from her calf and caressed the back of her knee. Pleasure of an entirely different sort careered through her. It left her shaky, confused. She didn't even like this man. How could she feel this way? Almost reluctantly she pulled away from him and stood. "Shouldn't we, uh, collect firewood, or catch some dinner or something?"

He stood slowly. She heard his slow exhale of breath. "I think I could use a little walk right now," he said so bluntly that Cassie felt herself blush all the way down to her toes.

"Is there something I can do?" She practically groaned as she said it. Quickly she added, "While you're gone, that is."

He grinned. ''There's a broom and some rags just inside the door there. You can clean up the place and I'll start the stove when I get back.''

She nodded and moved toward the cabin. She was going to need a few minutes alone just to get her wits about her. Her body was still humming from the feel of Slade's hands on her. She'd have to be more careful—it would be another day before they reached Mason's place.

And tonight. She stopped suddenly. She hadn't thought about actually sleeping in the same tiny cabin with him. But then, she glanced around at the slowly darkening forest, she couldn't imagine *not* having him there, either.

''Oh, Cassie,'' Slade called. She looked back at him. ''Watch out for the bats.''

He strutted off, whistling, leaving her to stare after him openmouthed.

Bats!

She turned and slowly lifted her gaze to the cabin's foreboding entrance. Was he just trying to goad her, shake her up a little? She shrugged off her fear, took a step forward and stopped. Of course he was.

Wasn't he?

Hesitantly she moved to the door and pushed it open wider with the tips of her fingers. Not a sound. Holding her breath, she shoved the door open all the way, then jumped back. She let out a loud sigh of relief. At least nothing had flown out at her—yet. Adrenaline pumping, she stepped inside.

The room was dark and musty, and the scent of damp wood filled the air. A black iron stove sat in the far right corner, beside a table with one chair. *Spartan* was the word that popped into Cassie's mind. This was where

Slade came to get away? She stepped into the middle of the room. A small cupboard with an assortment of mismatched plates and mugs stood on the wall opposite the stove. Beside the cupboard was a metal trunk with a sleeping bag rolled up on top. She shook her head as she looked around her. Amazing.

Slowly she looked up. The ceiling was high and open-beamed.

No bats.

She hadn't even realized she'd been holding her breath until it whooshed out of her lungs. One major crisis solved. Now she could concentrate on her next problem.

Where exactly would she—and Slade—sleep tonight?

It was dark by the time Slade finally returned with the firewood. He hadn't meant to be gone so long, but he thought he'd spotted the eagle he'd been tracking for the past week. He knew its nest was around here somewhere, he just hadn't been able to zero in on the exact location. His efforts had proven futile, though, and now, as late as he was, he was sure to hear about it from Cassie.

Light shimmered from the small window of the cabin, and he grinned. At least she'd been able to figure out how to light the lantern. He suddenly felt a strong pang of guilt. What if she hadn't figured it out and he'd left her in the dark? She'd have been terrified. He cursed himself and his thoughtlessness. But then, isn't that why he lived like he did? It was too difficult to be accountable to anyone else for his time. He was not, and never would be, a dinner-at-five kind of man. He'd tried that once and it hadn't worked.

The door was slightly ajar, and he pushed it open with the toe of his boot. The soft glow of the lantern spilled through the doorway. Slade stepped inside, expecting an angry tirade. What he found instead was Cassie, curled up, half sitting, half lying, against his metal locker, her head resting on a sleeping bag. She was sound asleep.

He closed the door behind him and quietly set the wood down by the stove. She'd been busy, he thought, noting the freshly swept floor and the lack of dust in the cabin. A sweet scent caught his attention, and he glanced at the table by the stove. Flowers. She'd picked a bouquet of purple mountain laurel and stuck it in a coffee mug. As he stared at the cup, a fresh pang of guilt hit him. Food. He'd forgotten all about food. She must be starving.

Slade knelt beside Cassie. Her cheek was smudged with dirt, and she'd pulled her hair into a ponytail, using a thin strip of cloth from a rag. Looking at her like this, curled up like a contented cat, evoked emotions in him he'd thought long buried. Feelings of need and want. The touch of a woman who wanted and needed him in return.

He ran one hand through his hair, fighting the overwhelming desire to touch her smudged cheek. "Cassie?" he called gently. She snuggled tighter and sighed.

He reached for her, wanting desperately to pull her into his arms. He caught himself at the last minute. He didn't trust himself to touch her and not want more, so he called her name louder. She stirred, and her dark lashes fluttered open. When she stretched and groaned softly, he swore silently and moved away.

"What time is it?" She sat up and yawned.

"You're the one with the watch, remember?" The cast-iron stove squeaked as Slade opened the door and threw in a few sticks of wood. "You tell me."

She squinted at her wrist in the dim light. "Seven-fifty-two," she said precisely, as if to annoy him.

Ignoring her, Slade lighted a match and had a fire crackling within seconds. He closed the stove's door with a loud metallic thunk, then rose and moved to the cupboard. "You have two choices for dinner," he said, opening the doors and rummaging inside. "Macaroni and cheese, or macaroni and cheese."

"Decisions like that always leave me so flustered," Cassie said, rising. "How about you pick?"

Slade turned as she placed her fists in the small of her back and arched forward. The light cast a golden glow over the delicate features of her face. Sleepy-eyed and rumpled, she looked sexy as hell, and he couldn't stop the sudden tightening in the lower regions of his body. The cabin had never seemed so tiny as it did at this moment. Frowning, he looked away.

"Slade?"

He nearly jumped at the sound of her voice so close behind him. "What?" he answered more gruffly than he intended.

She hesitated, then cleared her throat. "I was wondering . . . is there someway I could, uh, clean up?"

She stuck her hands in her front pockets and shifted nervously. He nodded, then mentally kicked himself for being so thoughtless—again. "Everything you'll need is in my locker," he said, gesturing with his thumb. "I'll bring you some water after dinner, then take a walk so you can have some privacy."

They ate silently and afterward, while Cassie picked up the dishes, Slade heated a bucket of water on the stove. Based on Cassie's nervous shuffling, he knew she was waiting for him to leave. He moved toward the door, then, as an afterthought, dug a fresh towel and chambray shirt out of the locker and threw them over his shoulder.

"Take your time," he told her, filling a clean pan off the stove with water. "I'll be awhile."

Cassie watched Slade close the door behind him, then released the nervous breath she'd been holding. She felt caged in this microscopic room with him. He practically filled the room himself, and she could barely turn without bumping into him. If this was what you called cabin fever, then she had a major case of it.

Not wanting to waste any of the precious time he had so graciously given her, she hurried to his locker and opened the lid as if it were a treasure chest. She nearly laughed aloud with delight at the contents: mirror, comb, soap, towels, even an extra toothbrush. Under the towels she found spare clothing and, hoping he wouldn't mind, she picked out a pair of black sweatpants and a forest green cotton shirt.

She washed, sighing in contentment as the warm water and soap wiped away the day's sweat and grime. She scrubbed her skin until it was pink, then washed out her bra and panties and hung them on a chair by the stove. She frowned at the sight, so totally out of place in this masculine room. Let him say one word and she'd strangle him.

She dressed quickly, then sat while she waited for him. Her feet, covered with fresh white socks, tapped a staccato rhythm on the floor. It was several nerve-racking minutes later before a sharp knock nearly sent her through the roof.

Slade stuck his head in the door. "Decent?"

She jumped up, nodding. "I...hope you don't mind, but I borrowed these from you." She held her arms out and gestured to the clothing.

The sweats bunched up around her ankles and the shirt, rolled up to her elbows, skimmed the top of her knees. He grinned at the sight. "They never looked better."

She smiled. "Do I look like a mountain woman?"

He stepped into the room and studied her for a minute. She'd combed her hair and pulled it back into a braid. "Maybe more like a mountain man's woman," he replied.

The look he gave her, hungry and dark, made her knees turn to liquid. She gave a nervous laugh and folded her arms. "I was starting to get worried. You were gone quite awhile."

He moved to the table to set the towel he was carrying on the back of the chair. White lace caught his eye and he stopped, staring at the feminine bits of underclothing. When he looked back up at Cassie, her cheeks were streaked with color.

"I thought I better wash up some myself," he said, dragging his gaze from the undergarments, "or you might wonder what crawled into the cabin during the night."

"I'm already wondering about that." She looked up at the rafters and hugged herself tighter. "Tell me you were kidding about the bats."

"You mean you didn't find any?" He looked up. "I guess I've finally managed to bat-proof this place."

Cassie groaned. She knew there'd be no sleep tonight. And that reminded her. She hadn't even seen a cot. "Uh, Slade, I was wondering, where are we going to sleep?"

"Where else?" He moved around her to the sleeping bag, unsnapped the tie holding it together and threw it on the floor beside the stove. "In my bed, of course."

Four

For a moment all she could do was stare at him. "You...only have *one* bag?" Damn if her voice hadn't developed a squeak.

Slade knelt down and grabbed the top end of the bag. "I said we'd share."

He pulled the zipper open and the loud, metallic rasp cut through Cassie like fingernails on a blackboard. "You expect me to share a *sleeping bag* with you?"

"Actually," he said, one brow raised, "I'm sharing my sleeping bag with you."

He was reminding her she had intruded on him and she would have to play by his rules. Still—she looked down at the "bed"—sleeping with the man was not in her plans. She remembered the blanket she'd seen in the trunk earlier. "I'll just use the spare blanket."

He sat down on the floor, untied his boots and pulled them off. Wiggling his toes, he closed his eyes and sighed. "One blanket won't cut it. And this floor is not exactly what you'd call comfortable." He knocked on the hardwood to emphasize his point. "We'll have to use the bag as a mattress and the blanket as a cover."

"Slade," she said, shaking her head, "I can't sleep with you."

Reaching over, he retrieved his jacket off the back of a chair, then balled it into a pillow and threw it at the top of the bag. "Why not?"

"You know perfectly well why not."

"Tell me anyway."

"Because . . . because I don't know you."

"Ah, I see." He lay down on the bag and propped himself up on one elbow. His eyes were steady on hers. "So if you knew me, you'd sleep here with me."

"Yes. I mean, no! I mean—" she threw her hands up and let out a sigh of exasperation "—I just don't do that sort of thing."

"Sleep?"

She stared at him through narrowed eyes. "Of course I sleep. You know what I mean."

"Look, Cassie," he said, his tone growing impatient, "this floor is hard and cold, the sleeping bag is soft. With only one blanket we're going to need some body heat to keep warm and—"

"Body heat!" She took a step back. "Listen, we may have to share a sleeping bag, Slade, but my body heat is mine alone." She folded her arms around her as if to emphasize the point. "If you get cold, I suggest you throw another log in the stove."

"I wasn't worried about me." He rose and retrieved the blanket out of the trunk. "I was only concerned about your comfort. If you weren't so afraid—"

"Afraid! Who said I was afraid?" His slow grin infuriated her.

"What would you call it, then?"

She hesitated for a moment. "Sensible."

He laughed. "Look, I promise to stay on my side, and I won't so much as breathe on you." Turning his back to her, he pulled his half of the blanket over him and scooted to the far edge of the sleeping bag. "How's that?"

"Oh, just great," she murmured. Her side was approximately twenty inches wide. A shiver coursed through her and she rubbed her arms slowly, telling herself it was the chill in the night air and had nothing to do with the fact she was about to crawl under a blanket with Slade. Her hands were like ice and she rubbed them together, then glanced around the cabin, still hesitating.

"It's going to be a long day tomorrow, Cassie," Slade said, his voice already husky with sleep. "If you really want to be sensible, then turn off that lantern and come to bed. It's no leisurely stroll to Mason's, and I have no intention of spending half the day waiting around for you because you're too tired to keep up."

She pressed her lips firmly together and clenched her fists. Damn him anyway! Would he ever cease provoking her? Fuming, she grabbed her own jacket for a pillow and turned off the lantern. The light from the softly dying fire in the stove washed the room in a soft amber glow. She stared at Slade's broad back, hesitated again, then drew in a breath and slid in beside him. She turned away from him, tugging her side of the blanket over her, careful not to brush any part of her body against his. If she stayed on her side and clung to the edge of the bag, she could maintain at lease four inches between them.

Why did she feel that four miles still wouldn't be enough?

Slowly her eyes adjusted to the darkness. Shadows threatened. She listened for night sounds, but the quiet was deafening. The floor was hard, she was cold, and her entire body ached.

How had she gotten herself into this? Here she was, in the middle of nowhere, lying next to a man she didn't even know. And though her thoughts should be solely on finding Sarah, it seemed as though every fiber of her being was focused on the man beside her.

She smelled the soap he'd used to wash, but the scent of the forest and a long day's walk still lingered faintly. The men she knew always smelled pleasantly of the currently popular after-shaves and expensive clothing. Slade's scent was entirely his own. It held a masculinity you couldn't bottle or buy. And it was much more than pleasant. It was absolutely and utterly arousing. She squirmed at the discovery and accidentally skimmed her calf against his leg. Electricity snapped in the tiny distance separating their bodies.

"Cassie?"

She jumped at the sound of her name then cursed herself when she heard his low rumble of laughter.

"You managed much better today than I thought you would."

A compliment from Slade? Well, almost a compliment. She smiled to herself and turned her head slightly toward him. "Thanks."

When his breathing grew steady, Cassie finally allowed herself to relax. She closed her eyes and snuggled against the blanket, amazed that she was no longer cold.

Slade was right. Body heat was a wonderful thing.

Exhaustion rolled through her, and the soft roar of the waterfall lulled her to sleep.

She stood in the middle of a sunlit meadow. Birds chattered on the high branches of a tall pine. Wind caught at her hair and she pulled it from her face, smiling at the antics of a bird that swooped down to capture a piece of the bread she held in her hand. At the far end of the meadow Slade appeared, his smile wide and welcoming. She called to him and suddenly he yelled, his smile gone as he ran forward, warning her. The bird screeched, raising its claws as it dove at her head. The rush of beating wings slapped at her face and she raised her arms to ward off the attack...

Cassie's eyes flew open. Her heart hammered against her ribs and pounded in her ears. Blackness was all she could see, and a momentary panic gripped her. With a small cry, she sat bolt upright.

"What?" Slade sprang up, his hand clasped on her arm.

Slade. The mountains. Sarah. She took a deep breath, remembering where she was. "I-I'm sorry...it was a dream."

His hand relaxed on her arm. She heard him fumble in the darkness for a moment, then the pump of the lantern. Still shaking, Cassie blinked and adjusted her eyes to the light. Shadows danced ominously over the walls and in the corners.

Slade watched Cassie clutch the blanket to her and stare wide-eyed around the room. Whatever the dream had been, it obviously had scared the tar out of her. Though he knew he was asking for trouble, he couldn't seem to squelch the protective urge that shot through him. Reaching out, he gently pulled her to him and enclosed her in his arms.

"It's all right," he whispered soothingly. "Nothing's going to hurt you."

Trembling, she grasped hold of his shirt and buried her face against his chest. "I'm sorry, it just seemed so real," she said, her voice muffled. "You must think I'm really stupid to act so silly."

"I don't think you're stupid." In fact, he was having a hard time thinking at all with her curled against him like this. His protective urges were giving way to much stronger ones. His body tightened in response to Cassie's closeness.

"Just give me a minute, I'll be fine," she murmured.

Her fingers opened and closed as she relaxed, and the sensation was wildly erotic. He gritted his teeth. "Take your time."

She could almost breathe again. The terror of the dream had passed, and her shivers were finally subsiding. She knew she should pull away. Instead she laid her open palm on his chest and felt the heavy thud of Slade's heart. Was she doing that to him? When she touched his bare skin where his shirt opened, his body went taut.

Slade cursed himself for his lack of control. She was making him crazy touching him like that. He started to pull away, but when she raised her gaze to meet his, he couldn't move. Her eyes shone with confusion. And something else. Desire.

"Who would have ever thought?" she said, astounded.

A smile caught one corner of his mouth. "Certainly not me."

"Incredible."

"Impossible."

"I'm not interested in this, Slade."

"Neither am I."

The words were barely out before his mouth caught hers, intending to prove them both right. It was a foolish endeavor, and certainly a dangerous one. The first brush of their lips confirmed just how much so. She tasted of pure passion. A taste so wild and darkly exciting, he wondered if he was the one dreaming, until her arms slid around his neck and she murmured something soft and heated. His hands tightened on her arms as he dragged her closer, deepening the kiss. He felt out of control, as if he were falling, and he held on to her, needing to take her with him wherever he was going.

She needed him closer. Cassie ran her hands over Slade's shoulders and through his dark, thick hair. Tension mounted in her, left her aching, and still she wanted more. Impatient with the blanket between them, Slade swore softly and yanked it out of the way. He murmured something, and the deep husky tone of his voice aroused her more fully.

Her world was dropping away from her. Time and space no longer existed. Only the insistent touch of his hands and his lips. His fingers tangled in her hair, his lips brushed her cheek, her chin, then moved down and kissed her neck. His breath poured over her like liquid fire.

Sensation after sensation pulsated through her. His tongue skimmed over her throat and she gasped at the jolt of pleasure that shot through her. Her eyes flew open and she clutched his shoulders, needing to hold on to his strength.

That's when she caught the movement out of the corner of her eye.

She screamed.

"What the—" He heard the soft flutter of wings before he actually saw it. He knew instantly what it was.

Bats.

One bat, to be precise. Cassie screamed again, nearly breaking his eardrum. She pushed away from him and dived headfirst under the covers.

"Cassie," he yelled, trying to get her attention, "it's only one little bat. It's more scared than you are." She had burrowed under the blanket, and he wasn't sure which end was which until she yelled back at him.

"I don't give a damn how scared it is, Slade. *Get rid of it!*"

Chuckling softly, he grabbed the towel that had been drying on a hook by the stove. The bat had settled on a ledge above the door. He approached it slowly, but when he got too close it took off again, squeaking. The sound of fluttering wings brought another muffled scream from Cassie.

This time the bat landed on top of the pantry. Slade moved quickly, and the animal, confused and frightened, didn't escape in time. Slade threw the towel over it, then opened the door and set the captured creature free into the night. He closed the door then moved back to the sleeping bag and looked down at Cassie's huddled form.

"You can come out now."

She threw the cover back and peered around the room. "You sure it's gone?"

He nodded.

"It won't come back?"

"Probably not."

"*Probably* not?" She ventured a few inches out of the bag. "That's real comforting." She glanced at her watch and groaned. "Two o'clock in the morning. Don't those creatures know when to sleep?"

Slade sat down beside her and pushed her tumbled hair out of her eyes. "They really are harmless, Cassie. *Myotis lucifugus*. They eat bugs, not people."

"Yeah, well, let 'myotis whatever' eat bugs in its own house." She sat up and her gaze darted nervously around the room. Her face screwed up and she gave a shiver of disgust. "Ugh. I knew that dream was a little too real."

He laughed and she raised an indignant chin. "You really do think it's funny I was almost eaten by a bear, then scared to death by a bat, don't you? Living up here in the middle of nowhere has given you a warped sense of humor, Slade." She sat Indian-style and faced him. "Maybe you should try coming down to civilization once in a while and checking out how real people live."

If the comment hadn't been so hilarious, he might have been angry. "Tell me, Cassie, just how do *real* people live?"

"Well, for one thing," she said, blowing a tuft of hair from her face, "we can travel from one destination to another with the use of a motorized vehicle called a car. There are roads and maps and people to ask for directions if you get lost."

Something that Cassie did a lot, Slade imagined. But he didn't say so. She was on a roll now, and he settled back, letting her go on. Besides, he enjoyed watching her. Her cheeks were flushed, her hair tumbled, and her eyes, wide with excitement, shone with the same golden brilliance as the lantern.

"And then there's this other invention called the telephone." She raised her brows in mock amazement. "When you want to talk with someone, you don't have to travel two hundred miles on foot and be trained in wilderness survival. You just pick up this plastic contraption and—voilà!—there you are, talking to that person as if they were in the same room. It's incredible." She shook her head to emphasize her point. "You just have to see it."

He leaned closer to her. "So is this an invitation?"

Her hesitation was proof she didn't know if he was kidding or not. *He* didn't know if he was kidding. She gave a short, nervous laugh, and shrugged. "Sure. Next time you're in Boston, look me up. I'd love to reciprocate the hospitality you've shown me."

He grinned. "You mean retaliate, don't you?"

She glanced around at her surroundings and then smiled sweetly at him. "Why ever would you think that?"

"A little bat told me."

She shivered at the mention of the furry creature and rubbed her arms. The smile was no longer on her lips or in her eyes. "Seriously, Slade. You really enjoy living like this? How can you stand this isolation?"

Maybe you like living in isolation, but I don't.

Those were his ex-wife's parting words. She'd come to hate this life, the life he loved so much. She'd come to hate him. He stared at Cassie, wondering how he could explain that the mountains were more than just a place where he lived. Besides, he thought, if he had to explain, she couldn't possibly understand. Diane never had.

Alone up here with Cassie he'd almost forgotten how very different they were. He'd actually been having a good time, and maybe he'd hoped deep down that she might somehow enjoy being here, away from the city and all the hassles. He hadn't realized that she was completely miserable. She needed conveniences: restaurants and shopping and beauty salons.

How could he have forgotten all that?

Her eyes followed him as he rose and moved to the lantern. "It'll be morning soon," he said, shutting the light down. Once again the room was swathed in darkness. "If you think you can avoid any more confrontations with ferocious animals, I'd like to get some sleep."

He hadn't meant to sound so cold, but when he slipped into the sleeping bag he knew his comment had hit its mark. Without a word, she turned her back stiffly to him.

He remembered how soft and warm she'd been in his arms only minutes before and knew it was going to be a long night.

Powdered eggs, canned potatoes and dried apricots.

Cassie stared at the food on her plate and felt her throat go dry. She glanced up at Slade, who was eating his breakfast with silent enthusiasm. She wasn't used to eating in the morning at all, and though the coffee he'd made would have been plenty, Slade had insisted. Something about carbohydrates and protein. And considering the mood he was in this morning, she wasn't about to argue with him.

What was his problem, anyway? she wondered, taking a tentative bite of the eggs. All she'd done was ask him why he lived like he did, and he'd practically bitten her head off. He never answered her, either, she realized. She swallowed the egg, then stared in amazement at her plate. Not bad, she thought, then cut off a small bite of potatoes. That tasted pretty good, too.

Why was he so touchy about the subject? She'd merely been curious why a person chose such isolation. He just didn't seem like the type to live alone. Not that she had a clue what "type" he was.

Then there was the kiss.

She was still caught in the aftermath of that. A virtual firestorm of sensation had swept through her. She'd allowed herself to go with it, to test it, expecting the fantasy to be more than the reality. She'd never been so wrong in her entire life.

The altitude must have seriously affected her judgment. She'd known instinctively that kissing Slade was risky, but she'd never dreamed just how much. And now that she had, could she just forget about it?

Of course she could.

"Would you like some more?"

His voice startled her out of her thoughts, and she could swear a guilty blush was busy creeping its way up her cheeks. He was looking at her so strangely she was sure he'd known what she was thinking. What he was looking at was her empty plate. She was surprised herself when she realized she'd eaten everything. "No, thank you." She pushed her plate away. "That was plenty."

He downed the last of his coffee. "We'd better clean up and get going, then. If all goes well, we should be at Mason's by late afternoon."

She scooted her own chair back and snatched the plates off the table. "I'll do the dishes." She stacked them in a bucket already filled with soapy water.

"Fine."

When he marched out of the cabin, practically slamming the door behind him, Cassie gripped the side of the bucket. She counted to ten, then envisioned herself dumping the soapy water over Slade's head. That thought cheered her, and with a contented smile she set about her work.

The pace that Slade set was grueling for a novice hiker. He knew that, yet still he pushed, anxious to see Cassie delivered to Mason and Sarah. This whole idea of bringing Cassie through the woods had been a bad idea. One he knew he was going to have to pay for very soon. A breeze ruffled the back of his hair, bringing a sense of uneasiness over him.

Seems like he was just full of bad ideas lately. Like that kiss last night. He was still kicking himself for that. He hadn't slept a wink the rest of the night just thinking about her lying next to him. She'd wanted him as badly as he'd wanted her, there was no question of that. He'd only had to reach out and ... and what? A quick romp on a hard floor in a sleeping bag?

He might be foolish, but he did realize that if he had made love to Cassie, neither one of them would be the same. The briefest touch of her lips had proven that to him. Her taste was already etched in his mind, drumming through his blood. He wasn't willing to risk more. He knew instinctively he could never have enough of her if they crossed over that line. He'd never be able to walk away after he'd left her with Sarah. And that was what he wanted to do. Walk away. Run.

So why was it then, he thought angrily, that all he'd thought about was kissing her again?

He stopped in a clearing as he realized he'd lost sight of her. Only moments ago she'd been no more than a few paces behind him. Or had it just seemed only moments? Had it been longer? His uneasiness increased. He narrowed his eyes, searching for a sign of her, then listened. Nothing. Just birds and the sound of the wind picking up.

He decided to backtrack, annoyed that she'd occupied so much of his mind he'd lost track of her. What was it about this woman that was different from others? She was attractive, beautiful even, but that wasn't what set her apart.

It was her spirit, he decided, watching a deer scurry across the path just ahead of him. It was the spark of defiance in her eyes, that determined tilt of her chin. He admired that kind of tenacity, the kind that had kept her behind him for the past three hours, uncomplaining. He'd known from the beginning she'd find Sarah, with or without his help. Though he still thought she had no business interfering, he understood her need to make sure Sarah was all right. If what she'd said was true, then once she saw how happy Sarah and Mason actually were, she'd leave and that would be the end of that.

Or would it?

He stopped and listened. He should have found her by now.

"Cassie!"

No answer. Only the sound of the wind, ominous now. Damn! He hurried, calling her name. Why wasn't she answering? She couldn't have gotten that far away from him.

But she could have. One wrong turn could have quickly sent her off in the opposite direction. He'd lost track of time. He thought it had only been a few minutes, but he wasn't sure now. He swore out loud. Violently. How could he have been so careless? He was trained not to be. He'd pushed too hard to get her where she wanted to go, and in the process he'd lost her. She was out there somewhere, maybe even at the bottom of a steep ravine. That thought sent a rush of adrenaline through him that could only be called one thing: fear.

It heightened his senses and sent his blood hammering through his body. The air had taken on a definite chill. He looked up at the sky and suddenly realized what had been nagging at him all morning.

There was a storm coming in.

It took him no more than a few minutes to retrace his steps and find the spot where he knew he'd seen her last. The ground there had been disturbed, rocks and dirt brushed aside, fern leaves squashed. Had she fallen? He called to her again. Nothing.

He glanced up. Clouds were moving in quickly now, carried by the wind. The same wind that was probably drowning out his calls.

The first fat drop splattered on his cheek.

He had to find her. Now.

Five

―――

Cassie sat on the rotting tree trunk, rubbing the ankle she'd managed to twist in an unseen hole. It wasn't a bad sprain, but that didn't keep her from feeling like a fool. She'd tried to keep up with Slade, wanting to prove to him she was able. After she stumbled, though, she sat down for a moment. When she got back up she must have taken a wrong turn.

That seemed to be the story of her life.

Sighing, she rubbed a persistent ache in the back of her neck. She knew Slade would be angry that he'd have to come looking for her. She'd cost them time and, by the way he'd pushed this morning, he'd made it clear he wanted to be rid of her as soon as possible. And that suited her just fine.

Didn't it?

Leaves rustled past Cassie's feet, carried by a sudden gust of wind. Shivering, she pulled her jacket on and glanced around. Ferns and lilies wavered. Shadows jumped.

Apprehension pricked at her like tiny slivers of ice. Until now it hadn't dawned on her that Slade might not find her. What if she'd gotten herself so incredibly lost even he couldn't find her? She closed her eyes, fighting back the tears. Maybe he hadn't even noticed she was missing.

Her eyes flew open again as a drop splashed on her hand and she looked up. Clouds were rolling in. Quickly. The air was heavy, tense. It didn't require a weather expert to know she was going to get very wet soon if she didn't find shelter.

She started to rise, then sat back down again. If she took shelter somewhere, Slade might never find her. Wouldn't it be better if she stayed in the open? She pulled her jacket tightly around her and listened for a sound, any sound, that might tell her he was looking for her. All she could hear was the roar of the wind in the branches overhead. Several more raindrops plunked down on her head.

She'd really done it this time.

Fear quickly evolved into near panic for Slade. He moved through the brush, amazed she could have gotten this far away from him. Anger at himself grew to new heights. Cassie had probably hurried to try and catch up, but if she was moving in the wrong direction, there would be a lot of ground between them by now.

If he was to assume correctly, she would veer to the right and follow the path of least resistance. In this case that was a narrow deer run. Twigs snapped beneath his boots as he hurried forward.

The smell of the storm lay heavy in the air. It was almost a tangible thing. Heavy drops splashed on his face and ran down his jacket. Even over the sound of the wind he could hear his pulse pounding in his temple. He called out her name, but he doubted she could hear. His eyes searched the ground.

There! Just ahead, he saw boot marks and moved quickly toward them. He could see no other prints, just the bent tip of a pine branch, as if she'd grasped it for support. Was she hurt? Thunder rumbled in the distance. The rain grew steadier, harder.

Think, man, think! He scanned the area. Which way would she go? The deer trail had ended abruptly, as they often do. From here on he'd have to guess which direction she might take. The wind swept leaves over his boots as he studied the ground. Instinct guided him and he continued to move to the right, toward a thick grove of trees several yards away.

That's when he saw her. Relief flooded through him. She sat huddled on a tree stump, looking utterly miserable. And utterly beautiful. She was in a clearing, open to the rain. Not a good place to be in a storm. When she saw him, her face, pale and forlorn, lighted with welcome relief and she stood, though unsteadily, and smiled weakly.

His heart racing, he slipped off his backpack as he rushed to her, then dropped it at his feet and closed his arms around her. "Cassie, I'm sorry."

He was sorry? She thought for sure he'd be furious with her. Yet here he was, actually glad to see her, pulling her close to him. "No, I'm sorry," she said. "I didn't see the hole and I caught my foot in it. It's just a little sprain, and I was able to walk on it." Embarrassed, she looked down at the ground. "I guess I just walked in the wrong direction."

"It's my fault." He placed his index finger under her chin and tilted her face to meet his. "I was so busy kicking myself over the way I'd been treating you I wasn't paying attention. This is my territory, not yours. I never should have let you out of my sight."

His words made her pulse flutter. His body was tense against hers and she leaned against him, welcoming the comfort he offered. As much as she hated to admit it, she'd been scared to death, and right now she hadn't the strength to fake bravery. She nestled her cheek against the hard muscles of his chest. His heart beat loud against her ear, the pattern wild and heavy. Had he really been worried about her? She lifted her face to his and glanced into his eyes. What she saw there startled her. Thrilled her. He really *was* concerned.

The wind whipped her hair across her cheek and lips, and he brushed the damp strands away. His fingers traced the outline of her lips. "God help us," he said huskily, "but we're asking for trouble."

His mouth sought hers with the hunger of a starving man. She met him, lips parted, feeding that hunger with her own. Trouble? she thought incoherently. It was more than that. Much more. Insanity. Bliss. Stupidity. Ecstasy.

She wound her arms around his neck, pulling herself closer. Desire swirled through her body. She feasted on the exotic taste of him, lost herself in the sensations that engulfed her. Rain fell heavily now, and still she clung to him, afraid to break the spell. He bent his knees and pulled her closer, more intimately. It wasn't enough. Lightning struck close by and he pulled away, his breathing labored.

"We've got to get out of this clearing and find shelter." He yelled to be heard over the storm.

Dazed, she nodded, allowing him to pull her toward a group of tall sculpted rocks. They were running now. The sky seemed to open, and another crash of lightning illuminated the forest. He practically shoved her beneath an outcrop of rocks.

"Stay there." He pulled a hood out of his jacket and tugged it over his head. "I'll be back in a minute."

She didn't want him to go, but the intensity of his words brooked no argument. She sat, bringing her knees to her chest, and waited. Several minutes later he returned.

"I've found us a home," he said, pulling her out from under the protection of the rocks. Water dripped off his nose. Carefully he led her several yards away toward another, larger grouping of rocks. Mud sucked at her boots, and the rain plastered her hair to her head.

Suddenly they were standing at the opening of what looked like a cave. A pitch-black cave. Slade went in first and reached his hand out to her.

She shook her head. "I'm not going in—"

He grabbed her hand, pulled, and she toppled through the opening. She shrieked, then landed on her backside with an ungraceful thud.

She wrapped her arms around her, sure that they were going to be eaten by an animal whose home they'd disturbed. God only knew what kind of creepy crawlies were in here.

"Slade, please," she said, "there must be something else close by. A cabin or abandoned shed or something. Anything but a *cave.*"

He laughed softly and produced a flashlight from his backpack. He swept the light over the walls of the cave and into the far back corner. "I've already checked it out. Nothing lives in here at the moment, and for now it's all ours."

"Terrific." She shuddered, following the beam of light. The cave was actually bigger than it looked from outside, about the size of a ten-by-twelve room. She scooted to the center.

Outside, the storm was in full force. Another crack of lightning illuminated the inside of the cave. Slade peered outside. "It's going to last for a while," he said with a sigh. He ran the flashlight overhead and spotted an opening in the rock. "As long as we can vent the smoke, we can have a fire." He placed a quick, light kiss on her lips and shoved the flashlight in her hands. "I'll go see about some wood."

Fifteen minutes later a small but strong fire crackled and warmed the inside of the cave.

Slade poked at the fire with a stick, watching Cassie as she removed her jacket and shook her head. Drops of water sizzled in the flames. He followed the movements of her fingers as she ran them through her hair. Firelight danced in the mahogany strands, accenting the red undertones. Her cheeks were flushed, and her eyes, golden brown, glinted catlike in the flickering light. Even dripping wet she was beautiful. Need rocketed through him, shocking him with its intensity. He knew she was saying something about the rain and her hair, but he couldn't concentrate on the words. "Cassie," he interrupted her. "Don't you think we should talk about what just happened out there?"

Her fingers stilled, and she raised her eyes to meet his steady gaze. The color in her cheeks spread, and she gave a nervous laugh. "Damsel in distress kisses the white knight?" Her tone was teasing, but her eyes were not. Passion still shone there, and it took every bit of willpower he could muster not to pull her into his arms.

"I want you, Cassie."

His words struck her like another bolt of lightning. She drew in a sharp breath. He'd told her once that when he wanted her in his bed he'd simply say so. She'd just never expected it to happen, so she hadn't been prepared. But then she doubted she ever could have been prepared for what was happening between them. She shook her head. "You said it yourself. We'd only be asking for trouble."

"It's already here, whether we asked for it or not."

It was true. From the instant he'd kissed her at the cabin they'd both known it. It was too powerful and too potent to pretend it didn't exist. Or to ignore. She glanced away and stared into the flames. "All I wanted to do was save my sister from making a mistake. Now it seems I'm the one making the mistake." She looked back at him and sighed. "So who's going to save me?"

As if to accentuate her point, lightning hit somewhere overhead, causing her to gasp. Slade moved beside her and took her hand. Gently he stroked her knuckles. It seemed as if the air inside the cave was as charged as it was outside.

"And just what exactly is it you think you need to be saved from?"

"Myself," she whispered. The slightest touch from him and already her pulse was racing. She pulled her hand away. "One-nighters aren't my style."

He stiffened. "I hadn't thought of it that way."

"Really?" She cocked her head and arched one brow. "Exactly what *were* you thinking?"

He started to answer, then realized the enormity of her question. He gave a short laugh and shook his head.

"Okay, so maybe I wasn't thinking. You have a way of doing that to me."

She felt the tug of a smile and tried to force it back. Neither one of them had been thinking straight. "Slade, it would be foolish to deny there's an attraction between us. We're mature adults. It happens."

"This has happened to you before?"

Never even close. "Of course," she lied.

He narrowed his eyes. He wasn't about to let it drop. "With who?"

"With, uh, Bobby Detweiler."

"And just who is Bobby Detweiler?"

"Someone I was madly in love with." She had a moonstruck look on her face.

He felt a tug of jealousy. "When?"

"Seventh grade." She could only keep a lie going so long. Her laughter died after a moment, and her tone grew serious. "Okay, so it's never happened like this before." She picked a twig off the ground and threw it into the fire. "The closest I ever came was a long, rather tepid relationship with the head auditor of my father's firm."

He didn't want to know about it. "What happened?"

"Well," she said, shrugging, "when we started talking marriage and he asked to see the last three years of my tax returns so he could calculate our incomes, I knew I had a problem. When he referred to potential children as 'delightful little deductions,' I knew *he* had a problem." She grinned. "I decided after that kind of fiery relationship I would be better off filing 'single' for a while." She looked up at him. "What about you?"

He stared at her quietly for a moment, then cupped her chin and turned her face to his. "I've never felt this strongly about a woman in my entire life, Cassie. Not even my wife."

"Wife!" Good God, she'd never even thought he was married! She pulled away from him, but he grasped her shoulders.

"Ex-wife," he clarified, grinning. "We were divorced two years ago."

She relaxed in his arms, at first relieved, then irritated. She had the strangest feeling of resentment toward this unknown woman. "What happened?"

He released her, then turned and stared into the flames. "One day she—Diane—made a trip into town and just didn't come back."

Cassie heard the bitter tone in Slade's voice, and she wondered if he still loved his ex-wife. The thought that he might filled her with an unreasonable jealousy. Before she could think, she said, "The woman was an idiot."

Her words startled him, and he looked up from the fire. "It's... difficult for a woman to live up here, removed from people and the city and family. There was nowhere to go and show off a new dress, no fancy restaurants that needed your credit rating just so you could make a reservation." He tossed a handful of pine needles into the fire and watched them burn. "It was over between us long before we divorced," he explained. "She went her way, I went mine, and I haven't seen her since."

Cassie sensed that though he didn't love the woman anymore, she'd definitely left her mark on him. He wasn't about to let anyone into his world again, or his heart. Why else would he live up here alone?

He smiled and tucked an errant strand of hair behind her neck. His fingers paused on the lobe of her ear, then slowly traced the column of her throat. Their eyes met. Outside, the rain beat a steady rhythm, but in the small cavern, the only sound was the crackling fire. Her skin came alive beneath his touch. Needing to compose herself, she closed her eyes and drew in a deep breath. It didn't help.

His hand slid behind her neck, gently pulling her to him. His lips brushed her temple. "In spite of what you think, Cassie, one-night stands aren't my style, either." His hot breath fanned her cheeks, and she leaned into him. "But whatever this is between us, I don't want to let it go without even giving it a try."

The kiss they'd shared earlier had been frenzied. Desperate. Now it was something entirely different. Soft and languid, undemanding, his lips caressed hers. The fire she felt deep within her built slowly this time. Desire flowed through her, unhurried. She touched his cheek, his throat, skimmed over his chest and felt the heavy thudding of his heart. The ache that spread through her was agonizingly sharp, yet sweet. His scent filled her: rain and woodsmoke, man and forest. She wanted to bury herself in him, lose herself to him. Forget that any other world existed.

His hands slid beneath her sweater and up the sides of her T-shirt. He tugged the ends loose and when his work-roughened hands touched the skin at the base of her spine she moaned softly and arched her body against his.

He wanted to speak, to tell her what he was feeling, but her mouth was doing something wildly erotic to his ear, and the words wouldn't come. Her skin was like warm silk beneath his fingers. He explored the curves of her back, then slid his hands forward along her rib cage. He wanted to touch her. All of her.

He stroked the underside of her breasts, and the soft rasp of lace caught in his calloused fingers. With deliberate slowness, he traced the outline of her hardened nipples with his thumbs. Gasping, she tightened her hands on his back and whispered his name. He wanted to take her now. Here, in this cave. Quickly and furiously, like the storm that raged outside.

Sparks popped off the fire and disintegrated in the soft dirt beside them. His fingers worked open the snap of her jeans, then dipped beneath the waistband. Her skin was hot and damp, and he wanted to taste her there. Everywhere. He laid her jacket beneath them and lowered her gently to the ground, struggling with the need to hurry. To make her his.

He was making her crazy. The feel of his powerful body covering hers awakened a primal need that cried out for release, sang through her with an urgency that shocked her. Frightened her. And, finally, brought her back to reality.

She stilled beneath him.

"Slade."

"Mmm?"

He pressed his mouth against hers, nipping at her bottom lip while his hands stroked and aroused. She'd already forgotten what it was she wanted to say. Maybe just one more kiss....

No. She placed her hands on his chest and pushed gently. He didn't budge, but he lifted his head.

She met his questioning gaze. "I—I'm not ready for this."

For a moment he thought maybe he hadn't heard her right. Until he looked in her eyes. Though still shimmering with passion, he saw something else there. Fear. A vulnerability that had him muttering a curse and rolling away from her. What did she think? That he would force himself on her? He sat up and dragged a hand through his hair, fighting to still the heavy pounding of his heart.

Cassie readjusted her clothes, then rolled to her side and raised herself on one elbow. Her body was furious with her brain right now, and she drew in a long, deep breath to steady herself. "I—I'm sorry, Slade."

"Me, too." He shook his head. "That never should have happened."

She stiffened at his words. She'd meant she was sorry she couldn't follow through, not that it had happened. "Don't worry about it, Slade. It won't happen again."

He reached around and pulled her to him so fast all she could do was gasp. "That's not what I meant, dammit. I'm not sorry it happened, and you can be damn well sure it *will* happen again." He softened his grip on her arm. "I just want you to know that before I brought you along, I never planned any of this."

She nodded, too confused by his words to say anything. Why would she think that of him? Hadn't he proven to her more than once she could trust him?

He touched her cheek with his finger. A tremor ran through her and she lowered her eyelids. With a sigh, he pulled away and reached into his backpack. "At least we're prepared for one basic need," he said with a grin and produced two granola bars.

He tossed her one and she caught it. She hadn't even thought about food. Suddenly she was starving. He dug in his bag again and pulled out a foil-wrapped package of dried apples.

"You wouldn't happen to have a blow dryer in there would you?" Cassie asked, pulling her tangled hair away from her face.

He reached in and pulled out a comb. "Next best thing."

She let out a cry of delight and set her granola bar aside. Important things first.

Slade settled back and watched Cassie tug the comb through her hair. Her skin glowed creamy white in the firelight. He could still taste her, feel the sweetness of her pumping through his veins. Not willing to torture himself any more than necessary, he looked away and tried to focus on his lunch. He'd lost his appetite.

When she finished she handed the comb back to him and he tucked it away. "Thanks." She nodded curiously at his backpack. "What else do you have in your bag of tricks?"

"Nothing you'd be interested in."

She reached for a dried apple and took a bite. "Try me."

He shrugged and reached in his pack. Carefully he pulled out two small glass jars and handed them to her. Squinting, she took one jar and looked inside. A large black beetle with a red streak up its back was struggling furiously to climb up the side of the jar. Without thinking, she dropped it.

Slade laughed and scooped up the jar. He tapped the side. "Not very nice, Cassie. How would you like it if someone dropped you like that?"

She shivered. "*What* are you doing with *that?*" She held up one hand. "Don't tell me. You collect them."

"Only the unusual ones."

She peered inside the second jar. This insect was green and skinny and had bulging eyes. "And just how do you know if they're unusual or not?" A bug was a bug as far as she was concerned. And a dead bug was the best kind of all.

"I had a class once in entomology. It was either that or psychology."

"You chose bugs over people?"

"They're a lot easier to understand. Nothing complicated about a bug."

She watched as he carefully tucked the bottles back into the bag. She honestly couldn't tell if he was kidding or not. Was she seriously attracted to a man who preferred bats and insects to human beings? Somewhere there had to be a short in her wiring.

It suddenly dawned on her how quiet it was. She glanced outside and realized the rain had stopped. Sunlight dappled the wet ground. She looked back at Slade. For one brief moment she could have sworn she saw disappointment in his gray eyes. A reluctance to leave. Just as quickly, the look was gone.

"Can you walk with that ankle?" he asked. When she nodded he offered her a hand up, then grabbed his backpack. He kicked dirt on the fire, making sure it was completely out, then moved toward the opening of the cave. "Time to finish what we started," he said, moving toward the opening of the cave. She followed, not sure if his words were meant to threaten or promise.

Thunder rumbled in the distance.

Six

A kaleidoscope of sensation struck Cassie full force as she stepped out of the cave. Sunlight burst through the scattering of high, pewter-lined clouds and shone like silver off the wet pine needles. The steaming ground glistened. Light-headed, she closed her eyes and breathed in the scent of damp earth and fresh-washed air. The wind, now a distant roar, swept through the treetops where an orchestra of birds sang and chattered sweetly.

Why hadn't she noticed it until now—this magnificence? It suddenly dawned on her why Slade had been disturbed when she'd asked him how he could possibly like this isolation. This wasn't something you could explain. You had to *feel* it. There was a sense of completeness here. Wholeness.

She took another deep breath and drank in the beauty, found it more intoxicating than any wine. Her knees felt weak, and she clutched Slade's arm for support.

"Are you all right?" he asked.

He stared at her, concern shadowing his gray eyes. She could find no voice, no words to explain what she felt at the moment. She simply nodded, dizzy with the splendor laid out before her.

He grabbed her arms. "What's wrong? Is it your ankle?"

"No, I'm fine." She touched his chest to reassure him, then turned in his arms and stared out at the forest surrounding her. "It's just that . . . well, it's so beautiful."

Cassie's words filled Slade with fierce pride. This was his home she was complimenting, what he did and who he was—his very soul. He pulled her against his chest, warmed by her approval as well as her closeness. He'd forgotten what it was like to hold a woman in his arms and share a part of himself. Her hair brushed against his cheek, and he drew in her scent, as fresh and vibrant as the cleansed air.

A need rose from deep inside him that had nothing to do with lust and everything to do with loneliness. Since his divorce, he'd thought he was content to be by himself—that he preferred the solitude. Now that he'd met Cassie, he was suddenly questioning that.

He'd misjudged her, he realized. He'd labeled her a wealthy city girl to the core. A spoiled one. She'd blown into his cabin hell-bent to see Sarah, determined to drag her sister home. By force, if necessary. A smile crept over his lips as he remembered her that first day, her eyes flashing, the stubborn tilt of her chin when he'd told her to get out. And the same persistence that had infuriated him then, he now found himself admiring.

When he started this, he never expected her to last. He realized now he hadn't wanted her to, that he would have found satisfaction if she'd given up. She'd not only lasted, she hadn't even complained. His smile widened. Except for the bat.

"I think I'm in love."

Her words startled him back to the present. She was staring up, caught in the beauty of a brilliant rainbow that arched across the sky and disappeared behind a grove of trees. It was a split second before he realized she was talking about the forest, and he had to remind himself to breathe again.

He smiled, remembering when he'd fallen in love with the mountains his first year in college, on an environmental-study weekend for a required biology class. It hadn't been easy to tell his parents he no longer wanted to be a doctor. To this day his mother said she wished he'd broken a leg or been chased by some wild animal. Anything, she teased, that might have kept him in medical school.

A bee buzzed close by and Cassie ducked closer into the protection of Slade's arms. He waved the insect off, thinking he'd face an angry mountain lion if he could hold her like this just a little bit longer.

"How much farther?" she asked. Her voice was edged with sorrow. She was no more anxious to leave here than he was.

"An hour, maybe two, depending on your ankle." When he held her, time was nonexistent. It dawned on him she hadn't even looked at that damn watch of hers once since they'd waited out the storm in the cave. The realization pleased him.

She pulled out of his arms, leaving him with an odd sense of emptiness and an aching need to pull her back.

"We better get going." She forced a smile.

He nodded and picked up his backpack, moving in the direction that would lead Cassie to her sister and out of his life.

Cassie stood at the crest of a hill and stared down. The cabin, nestled in a shady grove of trees, was no more than fifty yards from a small lake. The wood siding appeared to be freshly stained; repairs to the aluminum roof recent, she thought, noting the contrast of shiny against dull. Lace curtains peeked out from two square windows on either side of the front door, and a neatly stacked woodpile was conveniently located by the steps.

Not at all where she would have imagined Sarah sequestering herself. Sarah, who had always needed to be surrounded by people, who was the first to accept a party invitation, join a sorority or lead a protest. How could she be happy here, away from all that?

The peace Cassie had been feeling these past few hours splintered into doubt. She'd been lulled by the beauty, the serenity of the mountains and had nearly forgotten why she'd come out here in the first place: to take Sarah home where she belonged.

They were no more than ten yards from the cabin now and Cassie could hear a radio inside playing Janet Jackson—Sarah's favorite singer. The smell of something delicious baking wafted on the late-afternoon air. In a few moments Cassie would see Sarah, and the excitement made her heart race.

But first there was something she had to do.

She called out to Slade and he turned. She caught up with him and put a hand on his arm. "I want to thank you for bringing me here."

He looked at her so strangely she couldn't help the tremor of apprehension that ran through her.

"Cassie," he said hesitantly, "I . . . really need to explain—"

"Cassie!"

She whirled at the sound of the familiar voice and froze. There was Sarah, standing outside the front door of the cabin, her expression one of complete shock. "Sarah!"

They ran to each other and hugged, laughing, then crying.

Sarah loosened her hold and pulled back. "What are you doing here? *How* did you get here?"

Cassie wiped at a tear. "Slade brought me."

"*Slade* brought you?" Sarah stared wide-eyed at Slade, standing a few feet behind her. He smiled weakly and waved. Her gaze moved to the direction she'd seen her sister and Slade come from. She drew her brows together in confusion and looked back at Cassie. "And just how did you find Slade?"

Cassie stepped back and took a good look at her sister. Her blond hair was pulled up in a ponytail, and she wore a loose-fitting T-shirt and jeans. She was beautiful as ever and appeared healthy enough, though maybe her skin was a little pale. It was no wonder, Cassie thought, cooped up in a tiny cabin like this.

"Your letter was postmarked Cougar Pass, Sis." Cassie slipped an arm around Sarah's shoulders and squeezed. "It didn't take a great detective to find the place, though I was thrown off track by Mason."

"Mason threw you off track?" Sarah looked truly confused now.

"The *name* Mason. I got directions in town and ended up at Slade's." She glanced over at him and smiled. "I finally convinced him to bring me here, though I must admit, he's almost as stubborn as I am, so it took some persuading."

"No one is as stubborn as you," Sarah said, giving Cassie another hug. "I still don't understand how you got here."

"Through the woods." Cassie pointed in the direction they'd come from. She straightened her shoulders. "And except for the bear and the bat, it wasn't as awful as I thought it would be." She didn't think she ought to mention sharing a sleeping bag with Slade, or the fact she'd nearly lost all her senses and made love with the man. Those things might be a little difficult to explain.

"Bear? Bat?" Sarah's mouth was open, her eyes wide. "You *walked* here?"

"Well, you don't have to look so shocked." Cassie lifted her chin a notch. "I may not be in the best shape, but I can handle a little hike. Besides, I had to talk with you, and since I couldn't call you—"

"Couldn't call me?" Sarah repeated.

Cassie hesitated. "Slade said you didn't have a phone." She narrowed her eyes and glanced over at him. He was looking at Sarah. "You don't have one, do you?"

"Well, no."

She relaxed. "So, I wasn't about to sit around and twiddle my thumbs while Slade came to talk with you, Sarah. I had to see you, make sure you were all right." Bring you home, she added silently.

"Of course I'm all right. I'm wonderful." Sarah wrapped an arm around Cassie's waist. "Why don't we go in and sit down? I'd really like to hear about this little hike of yours." She shot Slade a curious look.

Inside, the cabin was tidy and compact, and Cassie was impressed with the warmth that emanated from the modest furniture and decorations. Cassie sat on a brown floral armchair, sighing with pleasure as she settled on the sofa cushion. Slade stood off to the side, next to a rock fireplace, while Sarah, seated beside Cassie on a small, rust-colored couch, listened to Cassie explain how she'd found Slade, mistook him for Mason, then followed him into the woods two mornings ago. Sarah gasped at the mention of a bear and giggled at the bat encounter. When Cassie finished, Sarah turned to Slade. He returned her steady gaze, his face expressionless.

"Well," Sarah finally said, slapping her knees as she stood, "you two must be pretty thirsty after all that. I'll get you something to drink."

Cassie watched her walk into the tiny kitchen and open the refrigerator. When she bent down inside, Cassie could have sworn she heard her sister laughing.

What's so funny? Cassie fumed silently. Did the altitude warp everyone's sense of humor? After all she'd gone through to get here, a little appreciation would be in order. And what was Slade's problem? she wondered. He hadn't said one word since they'd arrived.

Sarah pressed a cold can of diet soda in Cassie's hand, then handed Slade a bottle of beer. "Cassie," Sarah said, kneeling beside the chair, "I know yours— and daddy's—intentions are sincere, but you didn't have to go to all this trouble."

"Trouble?" Cassie leaned back and threw one hand up in an exasperated gesture. "Why would you say flying eighteen hundred miles, driving another seventy, then hiking through the wilderness for two days was trouble?"

"I told you not to try and find me," she defended. "I'm happy here with Mason, really happy. Nothing and no one is going to change that."

Surprised at the resolution in Sarah's voice, Cassie took a moment to consider her sister's words. "If you're so sure of that," Cassie said, taking a sip of the soda, "then why did you run off like you did? Why not bring Mason home so we could all talk about this?"

Ignoring Slade's snort of disgust, she set the can down, nearly sloshing its contents over the side. "You left school, for God's sake, Sarah. How can you just throw away almost two years of education to run off with a man you don't even know?" She hiked herself out of the chair and strode to a window overlooking a hillside sprinkled with yellow wildflowers. "We love you. How could you think Daddy and I would sit back and do nothing to stop you from making a big mistake?"

"Look," Sarah said, her mouth set in a thin line, "I may not have handled this whole situation well, but there is one thing I'm sure of, and that's Mason and me. We are *not* a mistake."

Cassie was taken aback. Sarah never showed any kind of temper, and she always backed down when confronted. Still, Cassie refused to believe Sarah truly realized what she was saying—or doing. "You like living in this kind of seclusion? Up here in the middle of nowhere?"

"Well, maybe not all the time, but—"

"Right. And what about your friends? And stores? You're the first one to organize a shopping marathon when Macy's has a sale. You have a credit card for every major department store in New York and Boston."

"People change." Sarah stuffed her hands into the front pockets of her jeans and glanced nervously over at Slade. It was obvious she was embarrassed by Cassie's report of her shopping habits. He was leaning against the mantel, his arms crossed high on his chest, his brows drawn together in a frown. Blushing, Sarah took a step closer to Cassie and said firmly, "Those things don't matter to me anymore. And besides, it's not as if we—"

Cassie shook her head. "That's what you say now."

"Cassie—"

"What about next week? How will you feel then?"

"Cassie—"

"Or six months from now, or—"

"Cassie!" Sarah grabbed her sister by her shoulders. "Will you listen to me? I'm not going to feel any different then, except I'll be happier than ever."

When Cassie closed her eyes in frustration and groaned, Sarah blurted out, "I'm pregnant."

Pregnant! Cassie's eyes flew open. "What?" Her voice cracked in the tense silence.

"I said—" Sarah took hold of her sister's hands "—I'm going to have a baby."

Cassie's eyes flew to Slade, ready to accuse him of withholding this from her. Based on his shocked expression, though, she surmised he hadn't known, either.

"Oh, Sarah, you could have come to me." Cassie hugged her. "You didn't have to run away and get married because you're pregnant."

Sighing, Sarah pulled away. "Look at me and listen closely, because I'm only going to say this once. I'm getting married because *I love Mason and he loves me.*

This baby is a wonderful gift of that love, and not Daddy or you or anyone else is going to interfere.''

Stunned by the quiet force behind Sarah's words, Cassie stiffened. She slipped her hands out of Sarah's. "Interfere? Is that what I'm doing, coming all the way here and then suffering through a crash course in wilderness survival just so I could see you're all right? I'm *interfering?*" Hurt swelled in her chest. "I'm sorry, Sarah. Maybe you're right." She stared at her sister through unshed tears. "Maybe people do change, after all."

Sarah threw her arms around Cassie. "Oh, Cassie, I'm so sorry. That's not what I meant at all." She let her arms fall to her sides and dropped her head. "I've really made a mess of things."

Slade couldn't stand it anymore. Cassie was pushing too hard. "The only mess I can see," he said, moving into the center of the room, "is on Cassie's part, not yours." His voice was comforting, but his eyes, fixed on Cassie, were as hard as steel.

That did it. Cassie stepped around Sarah. This was between Sarah and her, and he had no business sticking his nose in. She met him in the middle of the room and they stood there, glaring at each other like two prizefighters waiting for the bell.

"Who asked you?"

"Someone's got to protect Sarah from your bullying."

"Bullying!" She poked a finger at his solid chest. "I'll tell you who's a bully, Slade Mason. You! You dragged me through that miserable forest knowing I was scared to death. You taunted me and pushed me every step of the way, hoping I'd crack and beg you to take me back.'' She raised her chin and tossed her hair over her shoulder.

"I love Sarah, and I care what happens to her. If that makes me a bully, then fine, because I'm damn well not going to just stand by and watch my sister make a mistake without at least trying to stop her."

Storm clouds gathered in Slade's eyes. He leaned down so close his nose nearly touched Cassie's. "And I'm not going to stand by and watch you butt in where you don't belong."

Butt in! She'd never felt more like slugging someone in her entire life. She clenched her fists at her sides, contemplating one good crack to that arrogant jaw of his. "The only one who's 'butting in' here is you. If you can't see I'm trying to do what's best for Sarah, then you're as blind as one of your stupid bats."

"Oh, I was blind, all right," he said scornfully. "I really did think you cared."

Their eyes met, and each of them knew he wasn't talking about Sarah. Cassie moved toward him, wanting to tell him he was wrong, but she stopped, realizing that Sarah was watching.

Muttering a curse, he turned abruptly. "Looks like I'm the one who made the mistake." He slammed the door on his way out.

She started after him, determined not to let him get away without finishing the argument, then stopped abruptly. She couldn't just walk away with Sarah standing there. With a weak smile, she turned and faced her sister. A mixture of curiosity and wonder lighted Sarah's eyes.

"Is there, uh, something you'd like to tell me?" Sarah asked. Folding her arms, she tilted her head, her blue eyes questioning.

"No, of course not." Cassie slipped her hands in her back pockets. "Slade and I just don't get along very well."

"Hmm." Sarah stared at the door. "I guess not."

Cassie had no intention of expanding on the subject of Slade and herself. "Sarah, I'm sorry about the way I came bursting in here. I've just been so worried. You've had a tough time since Mom died, and I didn't want to see you in any more pain."

Sarah crossed the room to Cassie and put her arms around her. "We both had a tough time after Mom died. You just learned how to hide it better than me. I know I've done some crazy things the last couple of years, Sis, but this isn't one of them."

She sighed and pulled away to gaze into Cassie's eyes. "And as far as school goes, I just never fit in there. I never felt like I fit in anywhere until I met Mason." She smiled as she remembered. "He had a showing at a small gallery in New York, and he was standing off to the side. I got so caught up watching him watch everyone view his work, I'm still not sure when I fell in love, but it was somewhere between thirty seconds and a minute after I laid eyes on him. I invited him to dinner, then seduced him the first chance I got."

Sarah laughed at Cassie's shocked expression. "I wasn't about to let him get away, and I wasn't going to sit around and wait for him to make the first move, either."

Cassie sighed and shook her head. "You're only eighteen, Sarah. You still have so much time to—"

"I'll be nineteen next month," Sarah cut her off. "For the first time in my life I know what I want, and I'm not letting it go. You and Daddy are just going to have to accept that."

Martin Phillips accept anything less than what he demanded? Not on your life. Cassie suddenly realized she was going to have to be the one to break the news to him. The thought brought a sharp pain in her temple.

"Okay, Sis, you've convinced me." She slipped an arm through Sarah's and led her to the couch. "So how about we get down to business and you fill me in on all the juicy details of my future brother-in-law and father of my soon-to-be niece or nephew?"

Slade paced the lake's bank with savage enthusiasm. Damn if the woman wasn't infuriating! To think she'd actually convinced him that all she'd wanted to do was talk to Sarah, make sure she was all right. Cassie had pounced on Sarah like a bobcat on a rabbit. She hadn't even asked about Mason. As if he didn't exist.

Had she really thought she could barge into Sarah's life like that and entice her away with talk about shopping trips? Was money what it all boiled down to for Cassie? It certainly had been with Diane. He swore heatedly, telling himself he'd been a fool ten times over to think Cassie was different.

Talk about mistakes! He'd obviously made a gigantic one when it came to Cassie Phillips. And what *really* made him mad was the fact that even as he'd watched her try to intimidate Sarah, even as he'd stood nose to nose with her and resisted the urge to throttle her, he'd still wanted her. Like a raging forest fire, he'd felt the flames of desire sweep through his body and burn in his blood.

If he hadn't hauled himself out of that cabin, he just might have kissed her right there with Sarah watching. He halted in his steps, smiling wickedly as he considered what Cassie would have done if he had kissed her in front of her sister. That would have shut her up.

Or provoked her to murder.

No, he shook his head, that kind of rage was out of the question for Sarah's tender eyes and ears. Especially now that she was expecting.

That bit of news had really bowled him over. Mason and Sarah were having a baby. Incredible. Wonderful.

Diane had never wanted children. Considering the marriage hadn't worked, he should be happy they hadn't had any. He wasn't. He'd often times imagined teaching a son or daughter to swim and fish in a clear blue lake like this one.

He stared out across the mirror-still water. The plaintive call of a loon floated on the early-evening breeze. Maybe Sarah and Mason would share the kid once in a while—rent it out or something.

"Slade, you son of a gun!"

Startled, he spun around at the familiar sound of his cousin's voice. He came out of the woods, a canvas bag slung over his shoulder. Charcoal streaked the front of his worn jeans and chambray shirt.

"Hey, good to see you, cous," Mason said, grinning widely.

Slade forced a smile and clasped his cousin's outstretched hand. He wasn't quite sure how Mason was going to react to his surprise visitor.

"Everything all right?" Mason asked. Slade wasn't one to come visiting without calling on the two-way first. When Slade hesitated, Mason's smile dipped. He glanced up at the cabin and stiffened. "What's wrong? Is Sarah all right?" He started to move toward the cabin.

Slade reached out and grabbed his cousin's arm. "Sarah's fine. Better than fine, in fact. I just saw her, she's gorgeous."

Mason visibly relaxed. "She is, isn't she? I still can't figure out what she wants with a guy like me."

"Me, either." Slade shook his head. "I'm just hanging around waiting for her to change her mind."

"You're too old for her," Mason teased.

So he'd been told.

"Besides—" Mason's face softened and he glanced up at the cabin again "—you'd have to get through me." He looked back at Slade and beamed. "We just found out we're having a baby."

"I heard." Slade shook his cousin's hand again and slapped his arm. "Congratulations."

Obviously embarrassed by the sudden rush of emotions between them, Mason slipped his hands into the front pockets of his jeans and shifted his shoulders. "So, what brings you to this neck of the woods? You sick of your own mug staring back at you these days?"

"If I was," Slade quipped good-humoredly, "I sure as hell wouldn't come here to look at yours. Sarah's the only reason I'd risk life and limb tramping through the woods for two days to get here."

Mason's dark brows lowered. "You did *what?*"

Sighing, Slade raked a hand though his hair and glanced up at the cabin. "It's a long story. Prepare yourself."

Seven

They looked more like brothers than cousins, Cassie thought as the two men walked through the door. Mason was a younger, quieter version of Slade, with sharp, angular features and serious brown eyes. Eyes that were directed at her right now.

Sarah moved toward Mason and dragged him across the room to Cassie. "Cassie, this is Mason."

Cassie nodded, but made no move. From the expression on Mason's face, he would sooner meet a grizzly. Cassie glanced over at Slade, who was staring at her, his face set tightly in a frown.

Good grief, what did these men think? That she was going to haul Sarah out of here at gunpoint? The tension was so thick in the room you could walk on it.

Arms folded, she stepped closer to Mason and lifted her face to meet his unyielding gaze. "I have only one thing to say to you."

He stared at her, his face a rigid mask.

Slowly she smiled and reached out to take his hand in both of hers. "Welcome to the family."

Surprise, then relief, softened Mason's face. His lips curved up and his hand squeezed Cassie's. "Thanks."

Cassie glanced over at Slade. He'd relaxed, too, and though there was no smile on his lips, she could swear she saw one in his eyes.

"I understand you went through quite a bit to find your sister," Mason said, slipping an arm around Sarah.

"It wasn't all bad," she said deliberately, holding Slade's eyes for another moment before she turned back to Mason.

"I'm sorry, Cassie," Mason began, "I should have come to Boston and—"

"I wouldn't let him," Sarah interrupted. "He's on a tight deadline to finish three pieces for a show in New York the week after we're married. And besides," she said, sighing, "you and I both know how Dad is. I wasn't sure how far he might go to stop the wedding. I'm not taking any chances there'll be a delay."

Cassie understood only too well. When challenged, her father was capable of anything. And as far as he was concerned, Sarah was still his baby. What would he do when he found out his baby was having a baby?

"Cassie, you will come to the wedding, won't you?" Sarah asked nervously.

"How can you ask such a question? Of course I'll be there."

"And Dad? Do you think you could get him to come, too?"

Now *that* was another story. "Of course he will," she said with much more conviction than she felt. "Once I talk to him, explain you're grown-up now and need to make your own decisions, he'll listen to reason.''

"Listen to reason?" Sarah's expression was one of disbelief. "Are we talking about the same man?"

"Don't worry about it." Cassie squeezed her sister's hand. "He'll be there."

Sarah smiled and gazed up at Mason. Cassie had no doubt that she loved him, and that he loved her.

Now all she had to do was convince her father.

Nothing to it, she thought grimly as she looked at Slade. Stubborn men were her specialty.

She'd surely found heaven.

Cassie stretched one aching calf over the edge of the bathtub and sank down farther into the steaming water. Silently she blessed Sarah, who had refused help with the dinner dishes and insisted Cassie get out of the kitchen and go take a hot bath. She was relieved to escape, considering Slade had barely said two words to her throughout the meal Sarah had prepared. She'd also had the strangest feeling Sarah was carefully analyzing her company as you might a fly under a microscope. Cassie knew Sarah sensed something was going on between her two unexpected visitors, and she was waiting for an explanation. Cassie just didn't have one to give.

Sighing loudly, she closed her eyes, enjoying the heat of the water. Pure, unadulterated bliss. She couldn't even remember the last time she'd relaxed in a tub. With the hectic schedule she was on, showers were all she ever had time for. She'd have to do this more often when she got home.

Home. She couldn't wait to get there, she told herself. Cars and phones and people. Restaurants and shopping. Her own bed: queen-size, feather mattress, extra-fluffy pillows. Soaping one arm, she wondered if Slade had ever slept in a bed like hers. She imagined his long, lean body immersed in the mattress, his dark hair tousled from sleep. Would he wake slowly and lazily, or suddenly, radiating the same forcefulness that aggravated and attracted her at the same time?

What would it feel like to sink down in that mattress beneath his hard, muscled body? To feel his hands, hot and rough, against her skin? Would the passion between them be as strong between smooth, soft sheets as it had been in a thunderstorm?

Of course not. She chided herself for such a silly fantasy as she washed her other arm. They'd simply been caught up in the elements. Nature had teased them into shedding inhibitions. They'd been drawn to each other by the most primitive force of nature: He was a man, she a woman. Alone. It was really as simple as that. Once she got out of this environment, she wouldn't give Slade a second thought. She was sure of it. Absolutely sure.

She stepped out of the tub, wrapped herself in a towel, then indulged herself the luxury of a shampoo with a hand-held shower nozzle. She almost felt human again, especially when she slipped into a pair of Sarah's soft flannel pajamas and a fluffy white chenille bathrobe.

When she stepped out of the bathroom and into the living room, she was relieved to discover Mason and Slade had gone for a walk. Considering Slade had just walked for two days, it seemed rather ridiculous. Sarah, though anxious to talk with Cassie, was caught in the throes of early-pregnancy exhaustion and for love or money couldn't keep her eyes open. She tossed a pillow and blanket on the couch for Cassie, kissed her cheek and dragged herself off to bed.

All alone, Cassie looked at her watch. Nine o'clock. Good grief. She never went to bed at that time. But then, what else was there to do up here? She certainly didn't want to confront Slade tonight. She turned off the lights and curled up on the couch. The glow of a dying fire illuminated the room, mesmerizing her. Crickets, probably a million of them right outside the house, sawed in the night air, while frogs barked and an owl hooted in the distance.

She closed her eyes and drifted with the discordant symphony....

"Cassie."

Startled, she sat abruptly. Her blanket tumbled onto the floor. "Slade?" She must have dozed off because she hadn't heard anyone come in. It was too dark to see anything more than a silhouette of a man kneeling beside her.

"It's Mason." He picked up the blanket and handed it to her. "Can I talk to you for a minute?"

She glanced around, searching for a second silhouette. The sound of running water caught her attention, and she realized Slade was in the bathroom. Her pulse slowed and she breathed a silent sigh of relief.

"Of course." She swung her legs over the edge of the couch and combed a hand through her hair.

He was silent for a moment, as if searching for the right words to say. "I ... just want you to know that I really do love your sister. She's the best thing that ever happened to me."

Cassie resisted the urge to turn on a light. She knew how difficult it was for most men to admit their feelings. The fact that he'd wanted Cassie to know how he felt about Sarah was heartwarming. She laid a hand on his arm. "You don't have to explain to me. I can see how happy she is."

She could feel his smile in the dark. "I still wonder at times why she chose me. I won't be able to support her like she's used to, and I have to spend a great deal of time alone because of my work." He shook his head. "Lord knows I tried to dissuade her in the beginning, but Sarah was...well, determined." He chuckled softly. "Thank God she didn't listen to me.

"Anyway," he said, clearing his throat, "I admit I wasn't thrilled to see you today. All she does is talk about you. I know how much she admires you, and I guess I was worried I wouldn't be able to meet your standards."

"Mason, I—"

"No," he cut her off, "let me finish. I want to apologize for prejudging you like that. I can see now how much you love Sarah, and you were only worried about her. If it were my sister I would have done the same."

Well at least one man around here was reasonable. She glanced at the bathroom door. The water had stopped running. "In all honesty, I have to confess to you that I didn't think you could possibly be right for Sarah. Now that I've met you, I know I'm wrong. Based on the changes I've seen in her today, I'd say you're exactly what she needs. I think you're wonderful together." She kissed his cheek. "Sarah's a lucky girl."

He enclosed her shoulder with one hand and gently squeezed. "Thanks. I only wish your father felt the same way."

"Don't worry about my father," she said, sitting up straight. "It's about time he learned he can't always have his way."

Mason stood. "Thanks, Cassie. Sarah's right. You are pretty special." He leaned over and kissed her cheek. "I think I'm going to like having you as a sister-in-law, not to mention aunt for our child."

He turned and left her in the darkness. Aunt. She loved the sound of the word. Loved the idea of holding a baby, nuzzling its soft, round cheeks, protecting it. She meant it when she told Mason that Sarah was lucky. They were both lucky.

When she heard the click of the bathroom door, she quickly lay down on the couch and threw the blanket over her. Slade was the last person she wanted to see right now. She was still hurting from the things he'd said to her this afternoon, and at the moment she was feeling...vulnerable. Not a good way to feel with a man like Slade.

She heard him move beside her then hesitate. Her heart hammered in her chest so loudly she was sure he could hear it. He stepped away and quietly unzipped the sleeping bag on the floor. After a moment's rustling, he lay still. She slowly released the breath she'd been holding.

It was going to be a long night.

After two hours of trying to get comfortable, Cassie understood how Goldilocks must have felt searching for the perfect bed. Glancing over at Slade's broad back, she frowned, thinking her real-life fairy tale was complete with the big bad bear.

He was the reason she couldn't sleep. His presence filled the room. Three feet away from her she heard his breathing, deep and even. Peaceful. She hadn't had two winks, and here he was sleeping like a baby. She wanted to strangle him.

She wanted to crawl into that sleeping bag with him.

She cursed silently and lay there, eyes wide, determined to force Slade out of her mind. He wasn't worth the bother. He was overbearing and judgmental. Skeptical and suspicious.

She was falling in love with him.

Impossible. She shook her head, denying it to the darkness that closed around her like a fist. How could she possibly think she was in love with the man after knowing him a total of three days? It simply couldn't be. She wouldn't allow it to be.

She inched off the couch, dragging the blanket with her. She had to clear her head, get some fresh air. Away from Slade. She pulled on a pair of slippers Sarah had given her and crept to the cabin's door. Quietly she turned the knob and slid outside.

The crisp night air brought goose bumps to her arms. Pulling the blanket tightly around her, she moved toward the lake, drawn to the shore by the silvery shimmer of moonlight off the water. The woods behind her were pitch-black, but she wasn't the least bit frightened. There was so much to love here: fragrant pines, open meadows, lush ferns and clean air. Slade.

He was totally wrong for her. They argued way too much. He was mule-headed, dominating, obstinate and inflexible. She preferred a more...domesticated type of man. A solid, dependable man she could settle down with. Slade didn't even have a job. That sort of problem was bound to get in the way sooner or later.

But she also knew that once a man like Slade gave his heart, that woman would have no doubt she was loved.

Body and soul. She shivered at the thought, wondering what it would be like to spend her life with a man like that.

"Cold?"

She nearly stumbled as she spun around to face him. "Slade, for God's sake, you scared me to death!" She pressed a hand to her chest in an attempt to still her pounding heart.

"Sorry." His smile slashed wide in the moonlight. "I guess it's become somewhat of a habit to check up on you."

She warmed at his words. The blanket slipped down her shoulders and she pulled it around her like a shawl. "I'm sorry if I woke you. I thought maybe I could manage a midnight walk to the lake without getting lost."

He stepped closer to her. "I don't know, Cass. It's pretty dangerous." He searched the darkness around them. "There's some mighty ferocious animals around here."

"Well, so far," she teased, "the only one I've come across is you."

"I'm the worst one of all." He took another step closer.

Anticipation swirled through her like a hot wind. She gave a short, nervous laugh, then glanced away. "Slade, I'd like to explain to you—"

"No." He shook his head. "I really think it's time for me to tell you a few things about—"

"You don't have to tell me anything." She folded her arms and looked at the ground. "I'm the one who wasn't completely honest."

He stood there, his hair tousled, his shirt untucked, and stared at her, obviously waging an internal battle whether he should let her talk. She rushed on, worried that she might lose her nerve.

"When I first met you," she began, "I thought you were a pompous jerk, and I would have said or done anything to get you to take me to Sarah. There was no doubt in my mind I could get her to come home once I saw her. I never intended to just talk to her. I intended to bring her home. Not because my father had demanded it, but because I firmly believed she had gotten herself in over her head and needed my help." She sighed. "I didn't trust Sarah to make her own decisions. I've already apologized to her for that."

The distant howl of a wolf made Cassie hug her arms more tightly around her. "I can only say in my own defense that I felt I had to come on strong with Sarah. Assuming that her love for Mason truly was the real thing, then no amount of 'bullying,' as you so bluntly put it, would have changed her mind."

Damn if she wasn't making this difficult. He reached out and enclosed her shoulders with his hands. "Cassie, I realize that and—"

She rested her hand on his arm. "You're not angry?"

Only at himself. All night he'd been trying to think of a way to apologize to her, but he hadn't been able to get her alone. He'd come out here to tell her he was sorry—and to explain a few things about himself—but then he saw her standing by the lake, draped in the white blanket, moonlight spilling through her hair, and he felt a strange ache in his chest. She looked like a vision. An apparition.

But she was no apparition. Her fingers, smooth and warm, touching his arm, reminded him of just how real she was. Reminded him he'd already tasted her, that he needed desperately to taste her again.

Without wanting to, without meaning to, he pulled her against him. He felt the heat of her body, smelled the fresh scent of soap and shampoo. Her face lifted up to his, and as he stared at her lips, slightly parted and so damn inviting, he forgot what it was he wanted to tell her. It seemed much more important at the moment to show her what he was feeling.

He lowered his mouth to hers, more of a whisper than a touch, and gently savored the feel of her lips. Passion shimmered between them. His body tightened with need, yet he held back, afraid to let even one sweet sensation slip by him. He breathed in the desire, tasted the richness of it on her lips. Her soft sigh aroused him fully. When she rose on her toes and molded herself to him, woman to man, his self-control snapped. He sank his hands into her hair and pulled her head back.

Their eyes met and held for one electrifying moment before his mouth covered hers. His tongue explored the velvet smoothness, feasting on the ripe taste of her. He felt more than heard her soft moan. He pulled her with him onto the cool ground. Not even a thunderstorm could have stopped him now. He could catch a lightning bolt and send it back.

She felt herself falling, then rolling. A fragrant cushion of pine needles pressed against her back. The scent of clean, damp soil drifted to her. He wrapped the blanket around them, trailing kisses along her jaw then down her neck.

Her hands refused to be still. She moved them over his chest, following the corded lines of each muscle. Power and strength emanated through the smooth cotton of his heated shirt, and she grew impatient to touch the source of that heat. Buttons spilled open beneath her fingers and she slid her hands inside the fabric and pushed it out of the way. His sharp intake of breath inflamed her. Flattening her palms against his stomach, she roamed upward, circling his chest, sifting her fingers through the heavy sprinkling of coarse hair on his chest.

He breathed her name, then took possession of her lips with a deep, fierce moan. She answered him. Need, wild and raw, poured out of him and she drew it in, marveling at the intensity.

For once she was not lost. She knew exactly what direction to take.

Slade felt the gentle but firm push that Cassie applied to his chest. He complied reluctantly with her silent request and sat, pulling her with him. God help me if she's changed her mind, he thought darkly, releasing her arms. He'd never wanted a woman as desperately as he did this one.

She wanted him every bit as much as he did her. Her eyes smoldered with passion, and her lips, still moist and swollen from his kiss, parted with an unspoken invitation. She lifted her hand to the first button of her pajama top and tugged it loose.

He watched her fingers move to the next button, then the next, until his throat felt like dried moss. When he thought he couldn't stand any more, she slipped the top from her shoulders and tossed it behind her.

She was so beautiful. Moonlight washed over her golden skin. She straightened, tossing back waves of mahogany hair and exposing her bare shoulders and breasts. His blood hammered in his temple at the sight of her, her nipples pink and already beaded from the cool night air. He forgot how to move, how to speak.

He just stared, wanting to etch the image of her in his brain.

The pleasure Cassie saw in Slade's eyes excited her. She'd never undressed like this for a man before, but it seemed so natural with him. Everything about him seemed natural to her. She knew, with every instinct a woman possessed, that it wouldn't have mattered where she met Slade. Her attraction to him had nothing to do with the surroundings or environment, as she'd tried to convince herself since kissing him in the cave. An airport, a party, an office meeting or the Arctic pole. They would have simply looked at each other and known how it would be between them. The laws of nature would have prevailed.

She touched his neck with her fingers, then her lips. His arms came around her, pulling her roughly against him. The contact of their bare skin made her gasp. Her breasts pressed against his chest, and pinpricks of intense pleasure skittered through her. She murmured his name as she raked her hands through his hair and pulled his lips to hers.

A firestorm swept through her when he cupped her breasts. His thumbs kneaded and stroked. She arched toward him, and his mouth left hers, moving to gently kiss one swollen nipple. His tongue moistened and teased until she thought she might cry out. She grasped his head, encouraging him even as she wanted him to stop.

"Slade, please," she begged.

His breathing labored, he moved over her and gently laid her back on the blanket. He slid his hand over the curve of her hip, then under her pajama bottoms. She was naked beneath them. A low growl rose from deep in his throat. The bottoms were gone with one simple sweep of his hand.

Their lovemaking was as natural and untamed as the forest surrounding them. Drawing courage from the wild beauty, she touched his taut stomach then dipped lower, guiding his zipper open with trembling fingers.

With a curse, he pulled her on top of him. She slid out of his grasp, tugging his jeans over his lean hips while the peaks of her breasts skimmed down his chest and stomach. His fingers dug into her shoulders. She reveled in the sweet pain, came alive with it. Blissfully, achingly alive.

His body was taut beneath her, his breathing ragged as he helped her remove his jeans. Their bodies melded and he gently rolled her onto her back and tucked her beneath him. He stroked the inside of her thigh, then the moist, intimate center of her. She moved to a beat pounding through her. He grasped her hips and stilled her movements. When he slid into her she moaned his name and tried to pull him to her. He held back, resting on his elbows, taking her mouth hungrily.

A lifetime passed before her, then at last he began to move, and she clung to him, meeting his rhythm, increasing it. Tension built. Higher. Stronger. It grew until it consumed them, then burst into a brilliance as wondrous and beautiful as the sky above them.

Wrapping himself around her, he buried his face in her hair and spoke to her, but she couldn't hear over the pounding of her heart. She kissed his shoulder, tasted the salt of his damp skin. The wind whispered high in the pines, and silently she whispered too. I love you, I love you . . .

"Hey, sleepyheads, get up!"

At the sound of Sarah's early-morning wake-up,

Cassie groaned and buried her face deeper in the pillow. Good grief, she thought, squinting through her tired eyes at the cabin window, it was barely light yet.

Just five more minutes. She snuggled in the blanket. The sound of pots and pans and running water from the kitchen made her wince. Beside her on the floor, she heard Slade rustle in his sleeping bag.

Smiling, she lifted her head and peeked at him through a tangled mass of her hair. His eyes were still closed, his face peaceful and relaxed in slumber as it never was in waking. What was she going to do about this... situation? She'd fallen hopelessly in love with a man she barely knew. She had no idea where this was going, but as long as she was with Slade, anywhere would be wonderful.

It wasn't going to be easy convincing him, though. He'd made it clear he liked his life as it was: alone. He was not a man ready, or willing, to commit to a woman. She sensed his ex-wife's rejection had left him balking at the idea of needing someone again.

She'd be patient. She'd just wait until he came to the same realization she had: they belonged together.

Cassie looked at her lover's face, and his eyes, a lusty, smoky gray, were open now, focused on her. His slow smile made her heart melt and her body respond. Incredible. After their ardent night of lovemaking, she was amazed she could want him again so soon. And so badly.

She heard Sarah call out she'd be gone a minute, then the back door slammed. Cassie tucked her arm under her head and flipped on her side to face Slade. "You look like hell," she said sweetly.

His smile widened. "I'm not surprised," he drawled, his voice husky with sleep. "I went for a walk last night and a she-cat got her claws into me." He rubbed his chest. "I've even got the scratches to prove it."

Blushing, Cassie sat up on one elbow. "That so? Maybe you didn't fight very hard."

He shook his head. "She was the wildest cat I ever ran across. Damned if I didn't barely escape with my life."

Laughing, she reached out one hand to him. He entwined his fingers with hers. "You might think twice about midnight walks from now on," she teased.

"I have the feeling I'll be thinking about midnight walks a lot." He slipped out of his sleeping bag and kneeled beside her. His lips brushed hers lightly. "You could stay here a few days."

She knew how difficult that offer must be for Slade. "Sounds wonderful." She cupped his face in her hands and kissed him. "But I've got to get back before my father sends out the troops."

"I know a place we could go even the troops wouldn't find us." He ran his finger along her jaw, then X-ed a spot and kissed it.

She laughed softly. "If I don't get back to my job, I won't have one."

Stiffening, he pulled away and looked down at her. "You're awfully anxious to get out of here."

Slade felt like giving himself a kick in the rear. It wasn't that he hadn't expected she would be leaving soon. He just didn't like the idea she seemed so eager. But then, she'd done what she came to do. Now it was time to get the hell out.

"I'm not anxious, Slade," she said, sitting up. "But by the time we hike back and I catch a plane, I'll have been gone almost a week. That may not be a lot of time here, but in the city entire civilizations come and go that fast."

And lovers, too, he thought bitterly, rising.

She placed a hand on his arm to stop him, then kicked the blanket off and stood beside him. "Slade, it's not that I want to—"

"Morning."

They both started. Cassie's hand dropped away from Slade's arm as she turned. Sarah was standing behind the couch, a basket of eggs in one arm. How long had she been there? Cassie wondered with a silent groan.

"Sarah." Cassie felt her face grow warm. "I . . . was just telling Slade I needed to leave today."

"So soon?" Sarah's eyes filled with disappointment. "You just got here."

"It took almost two days to get here from Slade's. If I want to be back to work by Tuesday, we'll have to leave this morning."

Sarah turned her gaze to Slade. Her brows raised as she stared at him, as if to say, "Well?"

He shifted uncomfortably. "Uh, Cassie, I really need to explain something to you." He gave a halting, nervous laugh. "It's, uh, almost kind of funny if you look at it the right way."

From the pursed look on Sarah's face, and the guilt plastered all over Slade's face, Cassie had the distinct feeling whatever he was about to say would *not* be funny. She folded her arms and faced him. "I could use a good laugh right now."

Mason burst through the back door at that moment. "Hey, Slade, I just got a call on the two-way. That part for my truck is in. Get that lazy butt of yours up and come drive into town with me." Mason froze as he stared back at the three sets of eyes now trained on him.

He stuck his hands in his jeans pockets and hunched his shoulders. "Oops."

Slowly, deliberately, Cassie turned back to Slade. "Call on the two-way? Drive into town?"

"I was trying to tell you that—"

"Let me get this straight." She stood rigid, her gaze steady and hard. "We could have called here on a radio?"

"Well, yes, I do have a—"

"And we could have *driven* here?"

"We could have, but—"

She swung away from him, muttering a few choice words, then faced him again, hands on her hips. "You led me to believe there was no other way to get here but through the woods."

"I said it was the most direct route, not the fastest." Based on the furious look on Cassie's face, Slade decided he was about to die. He turned to Sarah and Mason for help.

They were gone.

He cleared his throat and faced Cassie. "I wanted to explain last night."

She folded her arms stiffly. "Explain now."

He wasn't sure he could anymore. He didn't even understand himself. Sighing, he raked a hand through his hair. "That morning in the woods, when you followed me and accused me of sneaking off without you so I could warn Sarah, I thought I might teach you a lesson and make you hike around the mountains for a few hours."

"A few hours! We were hiking around almost two days." She tucked her arms tightly against her, afraid she might slug him any second. "And just who do you think you are to teach me a lesson, anyway?"

She stepped back when he moved toward her. He stopped. "It started off that way, Cass," he said quietly, "but after a few hours I realized I wanted to be with you. I wanted to show you the mountains as I see them."

She thought she might crack open with the anger that was building inside of her. "So I was nearly attacked by a bear—a bear you *supposedly* didn't see—scared to death by a bat, slept on a hard floor and was almost drowned in a thunderstorm because you realized you wanted to be with me?"

His jaw tightened. "I'm sorry it was so awful for you."

"The only thing that was awful, Slade, was the fact that you lied to me."

"I didn't mean—"

"Just what did you *mean,* Slade? Have you so little to do sitting around all day 'watching the trees grow' that you consider dragging me through the woods a jolly good time?" She hesitated, then opened her eyes wide as a thought came to her. "That was a lie, too, wasn't it? Your cozy little 'getaway,' those bugs you carry around, knowing that a bat is myopic something or other. You're not out of work up here—this *is* your work."

He nodded, then sighed. "I'm a professor at Boulder University, on leave right now with a government grant to do a study on habitat management."

She closed her eyes, forcing back the tears. "Was last night part of your little game, too? Which lesson were you trying to teach me by making love to me?"

Furious, he grabbed her shoulders. "Dammit, Cassie. That's not true and you know it."

"True?" She pulled away as if he'd burned her. "I haven't a clue what's true. You've been up here alone so long you don't know the meaning of the word." She rubbed at her arms, trying to wipe away the need she'd felt when he held her. "Don't worry, Slade, I can handle it. We city girls are tougher than we look. I know there were no promises between us. We were both caught up in the circumstances, that's all."

"Do you believe that?" His hands were clenched into white-knuckled fists.

She didn't want to. It just hurt so bad to think she was nothing more than a convenience to a lonely mountain man she had to lash out. "I've got an idea. Maybe you could do a study on city women who don't want to believe a man could lie to them. I hear we're on the endangered-species list."

Slade's face flushed with anger. A muscle in his jaw jumped. He opened his mouth to say something, then snapped it shut again. Without a word, he turned and stormed outside.

Cassie turned and stumbled on Slade's rumpled sleeping bag. Tears streamed down her cheek as she muttered a curse and kicked the bag.

Eight

———

"These two applicants show the most promise, Cassie. One has more experience, but I have to say I'm impressed with the other's enthusiasm."

Enthusiasm.

Cassie leaned back in her chair and listened to her assistant's report. Enthusiasm. She stared at the Kilimanjaro-size mound of paperwork on her desk and sighed. Enthusiasm is what she needed right now in mammoth proportions.

"Jackie," Cassie said absently, "were you able to find out about the coverage on Frank Thompson's medical policy?"

"Frank Thompson?"

"In maintenance. He goes in for surgery next week and I want to make sure he's covered not only for the surgery but for the two months of recuperation time."

"Right." Jackie opened her folder and scribbled a note. "So this first applicant, the one with more experience—"

"Was that letter of referral typed up for Sue Yabroff?" Cassie interrupted. "She's probably the best compensation manager we've ever had, and I want her to have a great recommendation when she moves to California."

"You signed it this morning, Cass." Jackie slipped her pen behind her ear and grinned. "Right before you misplaced the file on impending terminations."

Gripping both ends of her pencil, Cassie stared at it. "Oh."

Jackie's triple-looped earrings jangled as she shook her head. She moved on quickly, listing next week's appointments, staff meetings and a studio shoot for the employee-of-the-month photograph.

Cassie stared at the potted philodendron on her desk. A spider was busy spinning a web among the leaves. Cassie leaned forward, wondering how a tiny creature like that could survive in an environment where it obviously didn't belong.

"It's a man, isn't it?"

Realizing that Jackie had leaned forward and joined her in staring at the spider, Cassie's cheeks flamed, and she sat up abruptly. "What?"

"On your mind. You know, as in the male species."

Cassie shuffled some papers on her desk. "I don't know what you're talking about."

"Listen, sweetie, when it comes to men, I'm the expert. I didn't work my way through three husbands without some experience. Ever since you came back from Colorado you've been . . . distracted."

Jackie was being kind, Cassie knew. Distraction was a nice term for brain-dead. If it hadn't been for Jackie's covering and running interference, every employee at Phillips, Weston and Roe would have probably lynched the Director of Human Resources. "I'm sorry, Jackie." Cassie sighed. "I know you've had to put up with a lot. I—I guess I'm just worried that I haven't been able to change my father's mind on going to Sarah's wedding."

Jackie leaned back in her chair and gave Cassie a dubious look. "Sorry, Cass. I know you're upset about your father, but I have the feeling there's more here than what you're telling me." She looked at her long, hot-pink nails and raised her brows. "Far be it from me to interfere, but I know the look of a lovesick doe when I see it."

Lovesick doe? Cassie chafed at the expression. "I assure you, it's not a man," she said a little too stiffly.

"If you say so." Jackie gave a sniff, obviously miffed that Cassie hadn't confided in her. "But if it was a man," she went on, "I can tell you all about what to stay away from..."

The conversation shifted from personnel to personal, and Jackie was soon lamenting the lack of a date this weekend for the clambake at the home of one of the firm's wealthiest clients.

Am I so transparent? Cassie thought soberly. She'd struggled for two weeks to keep Slade out of her thoughts, but her mind drifted continually to thunderstorms and moonlight, midnight hair and wolf-gray eyes. A knot formed in her stomach, and an ache settled deep in her chest. The plane ride home had been bad enough. In eight days, at her sister's wedding, she'd have to see him—and leave him—again. How could she suffer the same hurt so soon?

"Cassie."

"Hmm?" Jackie was frowning at her, and Cassie realized she hadn't heard a word her assistant had said. "I'm sorry, Jackie, I just...have a lot on my mind right now. Why don't you go to lunch, and we'll tackle the rest of this later? I need a little quiet time to finish this week's promotion appraisal reports."

Jackie's expression was skeptical. "If you're sure..."

"I'm sure." She smiled and waved her out. "Now go. Oh, and Jackie?"

Her secretary stopped at the door and looked back. "Yes?"

"Those two applicants you were talking about." Cassie gripped both ends of her pencil and stared at it. "Hire the one with the enthusiasm."

Grinning, Jackie closed the door.

Alone, Cassie sat back and sighed loudly. She was glad to have the work to keep her busy, she just needed to concentrate, that's all. Focus.

She picked up a file folder and wondered what Slade had been doing for two weeks, if he had given her more than a passing thought. Had it really been so easy for him to humiliate her like that? To lie to her and use her? Her throat felt strangely thick. She closed her eyes to ease the burning sensation, calling herself every kind of fool. She wouldn't let him get to her. She wouldn't.

Suddenly the door swung open and Jackie rushed back in, closing it behind her. "He's mine!" Eyes wide, she leaned back against the door. "I saw him first and you can't have him."

Stunned, Cassie stared at the woman. She'd gone crazy in a matter of two minutes. "What in the world are you babbling about?"

Jackie pushed away from the door and moved to Cassie's side. "He's headed in this direction, and if he sees me first maybe I stand a chance and he might let me bear a couple of his children."

There was a short but sharp rap at the office door.

"Quick!" Jackie pleaded. "Hide under the desk."

"Oh, for heaven's sake," Cassie said, shaking her head. "What are you—"

The door opened.

Slade.

It was like the first time she'd laid eyes on him—only without the shotgun. She felt light-headed, dizzy. Thank God she was sitting, because right now her legs were the consistency of gelatin. His eyes, fixed sharply on her, were stone gray against the deep blue of his shirt. His jeans were faded but clean; his boots polished a glossy jet-black. He was completely out of place here in this starched and stuffy accounting office. Wonderfully, beautifully out of place. The first breath of fresh air she'd had in two weeks.

Afraid she might jump out of her chair and run to him, she gripped the chrome arms and nodded at him. "Slade."

He nodded back, and she could have sworn she saw something in his eyes. Regret? Wishful thinking, Phillips, she told herself. Tension deepened the lines around his shadowed eyes, and his lips pressed thinly together. She noticed he was carrying a plastic bag labeled Boston Airport.

"You know each other?" Jackie was obviously shocked. Slade was not the sort of man who waltzed into Cassie's office every day.

Cassie nodded. "Slade, this is Jackie Miller. Jackie, Slade Mason."

"Nice to meet you." His acknowledgment was brief but warm, his smile devastating.

"My God," Jackie replied breathlessly.

Slade looked at her curiously. She blushed. "I mean pleasure, my pleasure." She glanced quickly from Cassie to Slade. "Well—" she drew in a deep breath "—I guess I'll just go on to lunch now."

Cassie said nothing. Jackie moved past Slade, sighed, then closed the door behind her, muttering something about never having children.

She sat back in her chair. "What are you doing here?"

The corner of his mouth tipped upward in a devilish grin. "You told me the next time I was in Boston to look you up." He moved toward her and sat on the edge of her polished oak desk. "So here I am."

That was exactly the problem. She'd spent an entire two weeks trying to convince herself she never wanted to see this man again. And here he was, shooting to hell every single argument she'd had with herself. It wasn't the two feet separating them that stopped her from throwing herself into his arms. It was the mile of pride.

Her phone buzzed. She swore silently and picked it up, answering tersely. "Yes?"

Slade shoved away from Cassie's desk, afraid he might give in to the temptation of dragging her out of that chair and into his arms. She looked exactly as he'd pictured her in her office: makeup conservative, her mahogany hair swept neatly back. She was dressed in a stylish navy suit and white silk blouse. Black high heels. Lord, how he loved high heels on a woman. He caught one look at those long, stockinged legs beneath her short skirt and would have killed to know if she was wearing the same sort of silky lace underwear she wore at the cabin. Would she taste different wearing lipstick, feel different here in her office than she did in the mountains?

Feeling like a caged cougar, he stood and wandered around her office, needing distance between them. He'd immersed himself in his own work the past two weeks in a futile attempt to get her out of his mind. It hadn't worked. Neither had the warning he gave himself on the plane ride over here: Just talk to her father and get the hell out, Slade. If you see her, you know it won't be enough.

So what did he do the minute he stepped off the plane? Headed straight to her. He glanced over at her, watched her slip a pencil back and forth through her fingers as she rested the phone between her chin and shoulder. All he could think about was pulling her into his arms and losing himself in her. He could imagine how wonderful she'd feel, how sweet and soft...

Letting out a shaky breath, he jammed his hands into his front pockets and forced himself to study the angular lines of a contemporary painting hanging on one of the office walls. No matter how he looked at the picture, it did nothing for him. When Cassie hung up the phone he heard her sigh.

"Slade," she said quietly, "what are you doing here?" She held her breath as she waited for his answer.

He settled himself back onto the edge of her desk. Faint lines of exhaustion beneath her eyes made him wonder if she'd had the same trouble sleeping for the past two weeks that he'd had. "I came to talk to your father."

Surprise, then disappointment, filled her. "You what?"

"Three days ago Sarah called your father, begging him to change his mind and come to the wedding. He flatly refused, telling Sarah that she was to stop this foolishness and come home."

Cassie sighed and rested her head on the high, padded back of her chair. She knew about the phone call. She'd been arguing with her father about it ever since, but his decision not to attend remained firm. Two weeks of badgering and cajoling and pleading hadn't budged him.

"I'm still working on him, Slade." A pinprick of pain centered between her eyes, and she rubbed the bridge of her nose with her thumb and forefinger. "I promised I'd get him there and I will. Even if I have to drug the man and tie him up."

Brows furrowed, Cassie sat forward abruptly. "But why are you here instead of Mason?" She reached out and grabbed his arm. "Is Sarah all right?"

He touched her hand. It was warm and smooth beneath his. "She's fine, Cassie. The doctor explained to Mason that a lot of women are more sensitive their first couple months of pregnancy, and he thinks that Sarah is just having a little bout with depression. Mason even offered to call the wedding off, give your father a little more time to adjust. He thought he was trying to help, but Sarah thought he'd changed his mind about marrying her. She spent the next twenty-four hours crying, and that's when Mason called to see if I'd come stay with her while he came to see your father." When Cassie's hand tightened on his arm, Slade instinctively stroked her thumb.

"Considering Sarah's condition," he went on, "and the fact that Mason hasn't finished a couple of his pieces for the show, I thought it was a hell of a lot more logical for me to come talk to your father."

Cassie looked down at Slade's hand covering hers, felt the way his thumb was caressing her. That's all it took. The slightest touch and her pulse was skittering through her like leaves in the wind. She pulled her hand away and smiled nervously. "The white knight comes to a lady's rescue again."

He frowned. "That's not the only reason I came, Cassie."

His quiet words brought a surge of hope within her, but she wasn't sure what it was she was hoping for. Her skin still tingled where he'd stroked her hand and wrist a moment ago.

He reached for her. "I need—"

The phone buzzed.

Cursing, he dropped his hand away and stared at the ceiling. Cassie took a deep breath and picked up the receiver. She told the receptionist to hold her calls, then hung up the phone and turned back to him.

"Slade, I—"

The words froze on her tongue as she watched him open the plastic bag and pull out a stuffed animal—a fluffy brown teddy bear wrapped in a red satin bow.

"As I was saying—" he handed the bear to her "—I need to apologize. I never got a chance to tell you I'm sorry I dragged you through the forest like that and let you think I was something I wasn't."

Slade's crooked grin melted her heart. Reason and logic told her she was probably setting herself up for another good dose of pain if she didn't walk away. Her heart told her to shut up and kiss the man.

She slid her arms over his shoulders and lifted her mouth to his as the door to her office flew open.

"Dad!" She stepped quickly away from Slade.

Martin Phillips stood at the doorway, his face a tightly reined mixture of surprise and anger. "What's this all about, Cassie?"

It took only a split second for Slade to size up Martin Phillips: a silver-haired, powerfully built man who commanded respect by his mere presence. His eyes— directed at Slade—were penetrating, questioning, demanding.

"Dad, I..."

Slade watched as Cassie struggled for some kind of an answer. Was this the same woman who stood up to arrogant strangers and braved the wilderness to save Sarah? Her distress unsettled Slade, made him wonder what kind of an overbearing, domineering father Martin Phillips truly was that he could turn a hellcat like Cassie into a frightened kitten. Anger simmered through him, pushing every protective button in his body.

He crossed the room and faced the older man. "Mr. Phillips, my name is Slade Mason. I'm here on behalf of my cousin, Howland Mason, and Sarah. I need to speak with you regarding your decision not to come to the wedding."

Slade's abrupt introduction caught Martin off guard for one faltering moment. His shoulders, as starched as his custom suit, rose. "I don't believe that's any of your business, young man."

"It is now." Slade held the other man's cold gaze. "Mason is like a brother to me and I've become extremely fond of Sarah."

Martin shifted his attention to Cassie. "Why were you in this man's arms when I walked in?"

Slade would be damned if he'd stand by and watch Cassie explain something that was none of her father's business. When she opened her mouth, he cut her off abruptly. "That, Mr. Phillips, is between Cassie and me. What I came here to discuss is Sarah's request that you attend the wedding next week."

Impatient, Martin folded his arms and turned back to Slade. "Why you?" He regarded his adversary with a cynical eye. "Why are you here, instead of this man my daughter fancies herself so in love with?"

It was a reasonable question, Slade knew. Martin Phillips would have no respect for a man who couldn't face up to his own responsibilities. Still, Slade had promised Sarah he wouldn't tell her father about the baby. "Mason—Howland—didn't want to leave Sarah alone right now."

Fear leapt into Martin's dark eyes. His controlled mask of power suddenly turned into the concerned face of a loving father. Dropping his hands to his sides, he took an anxious step forward. "What's wrong with Sarah? Is she ill? So help me God, if—"

"Dad."

Cassie stepped between Slade and her father. She'd finally regained her composure, though her stomach was doing flip-flops. Gently she touched her father's arm. "Dad, Sarah is fine. What Slade is saying is that Sarah is—" she searched for a word "—depressed."

"Depressed." Martin repeated the word with disdain and folded his arms. "Mason couldn't come here because Sarah is depressed."

It was not a word her father understood—or allowed—Cassie realized. The very idea was ridiculous to him. "Well, I didn't exactly mean depressed," she qualified. "She's just very... sensitive right now."

Good job, she thought. From depressed to sensitive. Another word her father didn't comprehend.

"Sensitive." Eyes narrowed, he gave her a sideways glance. "I'm supposed to fly off to Colorado and sanction my daughter's crazy marriage because she's 'sensitive'?"

Cassie groaned inwardly. Why did this always happen when she argued with her father? "That's not what I—"

"I think what Cassie's trying to say, Mr. Phillips," Slade interjected smoothly, "is that every bride gets emotional before their wedding. She's undoubtably under a great deal of stress, worrying that her father won't be there."

Martin Phillips turned to Slade and considered his comment. Stress and emotional females were definitely something he could relate to.

"What did you say your name is?" Martin asked.

"Slade. Slade Mason."

Her breath held, Cassie watched the two men. Like two powerful lions, neither one of them was used to giving in or giving up.

Slade extended his hand. Martin hesitated, then met the younger man's steady gaze.

They shook hands.

"Let's hear what you have to say, Mr. Mason." Martin laid a hand on Slade's shoulder. "I admit I am curious about this man my daughter's so infatuated with." He turned to Cassie. "We'll be in my office, Cassie. Have some coffee sent in, will you? My secretary's already gone to lunch."

Stunned, Cassie watched as they walked toward the door without so much as a backward glance at her.

She couldn't believe it. Her father was actually going to listen to Slade. Amazing. Shaking her head, she picked up the phone and asked the receptionist on her father's floor to take care of the coffee.

The man should sell cars, she thought, sinking onto her chair. He'd make a fortune. He was handsome, charismatic, intelligent...

Stubborn, judgmental, mistrusting...

The teddy bear stared up at her, its soulful beaded eyes pleading for a hug. Sighing, she picked up the fat, stuffed critter and rested it against her cheek.

Thirty minutes later, when Slade finally strolled back into Cassie's office, she had truly refined the art of pacing. Stopping mid-stride, her breath held, she faced him. "Well?"

He sat on the edge of her desk and eyed an apple she'd intended for her lunch. "Want this?" He held up the shiny fruit.

She waved her hand in annoyance. "Slade, answer my question."

A smug grin skimmed his lips. "He'll be there."

Relief washed over her. She let out her breath, resisting the urge to throw her arms around his neck and kiss him.

"And just how did you manage to accomplish this Herculean feat, may I ask?" Cassie couldn't help but be a *little* piqued. Slade had succeeded where she had failed.

"Well," he said, rubbing the apple on his shirt, "all I did was ask."

Ask? All he did was *ask?* Folding her arms, she fixed him with a disbelieving stare. She'd been asking for two weeks and had gotten nowhere. "You expect me to believe that?"

He shrugged and bit into the apple. After chewing thoughtfully for a moment, he said, "I also explained that Sarah and Mason were going to get married with or without Martin Phillips's blessing. It would be a lot easier to go and wish he hadn't, than not go and wish he had."

Frustrated, Cassie sank down on the edge of her chair. "Exactly the same argument *I* used on the man," she grumbled. She knew why her father hadn't listened to her. She was a woman.

"Cassie." The gentle pressure of his finger under her chin made her look up. He set the apple down. "What's important is he's coming. Right?"

At this moment, with Slade touching her, leaning so close to her she could breathe in the mingled scent of apple and some dark, musky fragrance of after-shave, she was having a hard time remembering what was or wasn't important. Like pride, and not burning herself on the same frying pan twice.

Her pulse beat wildly in her throat. "You're right, of course." Managing a weak smile, she whispered, "That's all that matters."

He stared at her for a long moment, then, with almost a growl, he pulled her to him. His mouth covered hers, hungry and demanding. Insistent. Her hands went to his chest, intending to push him away. She pulled him closer, cursing herself for her weakness. Her body came alive beneath his touch, and when he murmured her name, sparks skimmed over her skin. Need was sharp and instantaneous. Her breasts tightened, aching to be touched, stroked, kissed.

He broke away from her and stood, leaving her dazed and weak. Empty.

He moved to the window and stared out at the city below. She heard his sharp intake of breath then weary sigh. "Cassie, I have a six-thirty flight out of here tonight."

Six-thirty flight? She looked at him, confused. "You aren't staying?"

He shook his head. "I can't."

Can't, or didn't want to? How could he kiss her like that then casually tell her he was leaving in a few hours? She turned away from him, feeling as if she might break into a thousand pieces.

So he really had come just to speak with her father. And to ease his guilty conscience because he lied to her in the mountains. Her eyes burned with unshed tears. What a fool she was to think he might have come to see her, to be with her. He'd made it clear he enjoyed his life the way it was: alone and uncomplicated. Why should she have thought he had changed his mind now?

But she knew, even if he didn't yet, that he loved her. She felt it in his touch, saw it in his eyes. He was afraid of falling in love again. He was determined to shut her out of his life rather than take the chance.

She was determined to give it her best shot to find a way in.

"Well, then," she said, turning back to him, "I suggest we make the most of the few hours we do have."

Nine

"You call that a bed?"

Standing behind Cassie, Slade leaned close and whispered the words in her ear. She shifted nervously, and he wondered if she was having second thoughts about bringing him here.

"It's a beautiful bed," she defended, lifting her chin a notch. "Simple, maybe, but utilitarian." She glanced over her shoulder at him, and mischief danced in her honey-golden eyes. "And certainly more comfortable than a sleeping bag."

He looked back, not sure if he believed her. "Paul Revere, huh?"

She nodded. "The one and only."

They both stared at the bed as the tour guide's voice droned on, explaining life in eighteenth-century Boston to the group of tourists crowded in the small bedroom of one of the country's most famous defenders.

Slade didn't hear a word. He was too intent on Cassie. He couldn't help but appreciate the long stretch of bare legs beneath the pink shorts she'd changed into at work, and her T-shirt, white with blue tulips and a Boston insignia, clung to her damp skin. Tiny drops of perspiration gathered on her upper lip. He checked the impulse to wipe them away with his thumb, and dug his hands into his pockets, forcing himself to listen to the guide.

"...the oldest house in Boston, Paul Revere lived here from 1770 to 1800..."

Because her office was so close, and because midday traffic was at a standstill, they had walked everywhere: a park with swan boats, a three-hundred-year-old church, old city hall, the site of the Boston massacre. He couldn't deny it was a beautiful city, rich with history, abundant with exquisite architecture and finely crafted statues.

But it was still the city. A hot and humid one.

When she leaned back against him, allowing a tourist to take a picture, Slade felt his entire body go taut. Since he'd kissed her this morning, he'd avoided touching her again, afraid if he did, he'd lose all control. It was better this way, he told himself, keeping his hands stiffly at his sides.

Cassie's shoulder pressed against his chest, and the need to hold her coiled in him as tightly as a watch spring. The room closed in on him. He swiped at the moistness on his forehead, closing his wet palms into fists as he glanced down at her. Strands of damp hair curled around her flushed face. She'd set a whirlwind pace to show him Boston, and right now she looked as though she were about to collapse. He took her by the arm.

"Let's get out of here and get something to eat," he said, pulling her away from the group. Relief lighted her face. Once outside, with some distance between them again, Slade felt relieved, as well.

A short walk and several minutes later he followed her into Faneuil Hall, a large, rectangular-shaped warehouse lined on each side with concession stands.

The smell of pizza and sausage and spices filled the air. Bakeries pulled fresh loaves of bread from their ovens, and candy booths simmered melted chocolate in large vats. Slade ordered sub sandwiches and sodas, then worked his way through the crowd of patrons back to Cassie, who waited for him off to one side.

"There's no place to sit right now." She had to practically yell to be heard over the roar of voices. She pointed to an empty counter on the wall opposite them.

So much for some quiet time together, Slade growled silently. He knew that was the wisest thing, so why did he feel like he was twisted up in one giant knot? They had less than four hours together. It wasn't enough, and every time Cassie checked her watch it reminded him of that fact.

Since conversation was almost impossible, he watched the people around him: two little boys fighting over a hand-held catsup dispenser, an elderly couple studying a map, a businessman reading a paper.

Slade stiffened. The man *wasn't* reading his paper.

He was staring at Cassie.

Slade felt the hair bristle on the back of his neck. His jaw tightened. He didn't like anyone else looking at Cassie. Especially not the way this man was—like he wanted to take her to bed. He looked exactly like the type Slade imagined Cassie dated. A lawyer, or maybe an investment broker who modeled for clothing catalogs in his spare time.

When the man staring at Cassie realized Slade was watching him, he quickly looked away. Good thing for him, Slade thought. He'd been trying to decide which way to bend the guy's nose.

"What's wrong?" Cassie said loudly in his ear.

"Nothing." He snapped the words. How could he tell her he was suddenly, and irrationally, jealous, that he couldn't stand the idea of her seeing other men, and the mere thought of another man kissing her, touching her, was eating up his insides? He had no right.

Cassie studied Slade's face. His eyes, as dark and angry as thunderclouds, were narrowed as he stared across the room. She followed his gaze, but only saw a man reading a paper.

"Nothing?" she snapped right back at him. "All afternoon you've had a major chip on your shoulder you've been begging someone to knock off. Don't tell me nothing's wrong."

She'd wanted these last few hours they had together to be perfect, but all her plans had gone to hell. His taciturn attitude, mixed with the fact that he hadn't touched her once—even though she'd made sure he'd had plenty of opportunity—were stretching her patience to the breaking point. She was hot and miserable and trying to forget that the man she loved was walking out of her life in a few hours. Her entire body ached with that knowledge.

When he continued to frown without saying a word, she decided she'd had enough. "Maybe this was a bad idea, Slade." She laid her sandwich down and wrapped it up. "You've been like a lion on a leash all afternoon. If you don't want to be with me, just say so. There are plenty of taxis to the airport, and I have a desk full of work waiting for me."

What in the world was she talking about? He stared at her for a moment, too stunned to respond. Not want to be with her? He couldn't stand the thought of *not* being with her.

"I think the heat's gotten to you, Cassie," he drawled lazily. "You're the one checking your watch every five minutes like you can't wait to get rid of me. And as far as your work, I wasn't the one who suggested you take the afternoon off and we do the *Reader's Digest* condensed version of Boston in an afternoon."

That cut deep. Too deep. Hurt welled up inside of her and made her take a step back. "I wanted to show you Boston," she said quietly, so quietly she didn't even know if he could hear her over the noise of the hall. "I wanted to show you some of the beauty we have here, like you showed me in the mountains. I wanted you to feel, if only a little, some of the magic we have here, too." She turned her head and blinked back the tears. "If I was looking at my watch, it was because I was afraid of losing even a few minutes of the time we have together."

He hadn't meant to hurt her. He'd been so wrapped up in his own feelings he hadn't realized he'd been acting like an idiot. He grabbed her arm as she started to turn away. "Cassie, I'm sorry." She wouldn't look at him, but she wasn't pulling away. "Boston is beautiful. That's not the problem."

She shook off his hand. "So what is it then?"

He almost laughed. *That* was a good question. His throat suddenly felt like sawdust, and he picked up his soda, wishing it were something stronger. "I—I'm having a hell of a time trying to—"

A small, squealing body came at him, bumping his arm as it raced by, spilling the entire contents of his drink down the front of him. A second compact body followed the first, squirting catsup from a plastic dispenser, missing his intended victim and striking Slade smack-dab above the crotch of his jeans.

Shock froze Slade's startled expression. He stood there, stock-still, and slowly lowered his gaze. Catsup, mixed with dripping soda, oozed down the front of his pants. His shirt was drenched and plastered to his chest.

"Bobby! Jonathan!" a woman shrieked at the two boys. "Just look what you've done." The woman tore a handful of napkins from a dispenser and dabbed at Slade's chest. When she started to move lower, he snatched the napkins from her.

"I'm so sorry, so terribly sorry," she wailed, then, with narrowed eyes, turned on her children. Fear illuminated her sons' faces. As they started to run off, she grabbed them by the scruffs of their shirts and dragged them back to stand in front of Slade.

"If you send me the bill, I'll be happy to—"

Slade waved a hand. "Never mind," he said flatly, accepting the fresh batch of napkins Cassie thrust at him. "I'll manage."

"Say you're sorry to the man," the mother reprimanded, giving her sons a quick shake. Their heads hanging, the boys mumbled an apology, then were promptly dragged off with promises of punishment.

Cassie stared at the front of Slade's jeans. Catsup streaked his midsection. "I really don't think I can help you with this." She was trying not to laugh.

He mopped at himself. It only smeared worse. "I look like someone took a chain saw to me."

Cassie sighed, folding her arms as she studied the mess. "Well, Slade, you've got no choice now." She picked up her purse and shook her head. "Looks like you're coming home with me."

Stark naked, Slade stood in the middle of Cassie's bathroom. Clouds of steam rolled out from the shower stall. He touched his chest and grimaced, not only because it was sticky, but because he knew he reeked of dried soda and catsup.

"Need anything?" he heard Cassie call from the other side of the door where she was picking up the clothes he'd tossed into the hall.

Her. The thought came to him before he could stop it. But what he needed and what he could have were two different things. "Just a towel."

"I have extra in the linen closet beside the shower."

There was a momentary silence, and he thought maybe she'd walked away. He had the most incredible urge to throw open the door and drag her back in here with him. He reached for the doorknob, then froze when she spoke again. "I'm going to toss these things in the washer, Slade," she called through the door. "I'll be back."

He took a deep breath to steady himself. "Take your time," he mumbled.

Get a grip, he chastised himself when she'd left. Though he wanted nothing more than to be with Cassie, he knew it would only be harder for her when he left in a few hours.

Slade looked around the bathroom, noting it was twice the size of his, with a tub separate from the over-size shower stall. His feet sank in the thick, deep blue carpeting. Decorator towels, clean and plush, hung on a gold-toned bar beside the shower.

He opened the shower door and stepped beneath the hard spray of hot water. He could smell her in here, her soap, her shampoo. The thought of never seeing her again twisted in his gut like a fist.

Snatching up a bar of soap, he scrubbed furiously at his chest and his arms. Oh, he'd see her all right—in a week at the wedding just for starters. After that, they were bound to run into each other occasionally. That thought gave him no solace, only deepened the clawing in his stomach. It wouldn't be enough, just seeing her. He needed so much more than that: her body cradled next to his in the morning, her jacket on his coat hook when he came home at night. Her toothbrush next to his.

He gritted his teeth and turned the faucet to cold.

It was easier this way. They wouldn't have to argue over the long hours he put in when he was on a project. Sometimes he was gone for days. She'd resent the fact that they couldn't run out to a movie or a restaurant on a whim. She'd never be happy in the mountains, and he couldn't stand the thought of Cassie not being happy.

Slade closed his eyes and shoved his head under the blast of water. He stood there, breath held, hoping the cold water might clear his head and ease the ache in his chest.

That's when he heard the shower door open.

Startled, he looked up and froze.

Cassie stood just outside the shower, her hand hesitant on the glass door. She'd wrapped a fluffy blue towel around her, but underneath he knew she was beautifully, gloriously, naked. Her eyes, wide with ap-

prehension, locked onto his. She made no step toward
him. Her back straight, shoulders squared, she waited.

His move.

He was too stunned to speak. Need tore at him,
shredding his resistance as if it were thin paper. He
looked at her, wanting her as he'd never wanted another woman; as he knew he would never want another
woman again. A tremor broke loose in him and worked
its way up his taut body. Spellbound, he watched as
uncertainty filled her gaze just before her thick lashes
fluttered down and she let out a faltering breath.

Cassie felt her insides crumble bit by bit as Slade just
stared at her. What had she been thinking, anyway?
That she could just throw herself at him and he'd fall at
her feet, professing his eternal love?

Maybe that was what she'd hoped for, idiot that she
was. Though he'd never said so, she'd truly thought that
deep down he loved her as much as she loved him. She'd
obviously been wrong.

Unable to bear his rejection another moment, she
glanced at her toes, wishing she could disappear down
the shower drain. It was humiliating, standing here with
nothing more than a towel on. But her embarrassment
was nothing compared to the pain that engulfed her.
Her knees were shaking so badly she knew she wouldn't
even be able to manage a dignified retreat.

She started to turn when his wet hand caught hers.

"Cassie."

She kept her eyes on the floor, on her own feet; anywhere but on him. He pulled her gently to the edge of
the shower. She steeled herself, expecting him to say,
Thanks, but no thanks.

He stepped closer. His hand moved up her arm and
his knuckles brushed lightly where the towel ended and

skin began. Her heart beat loud and hard, like a child
on a drum. His hand turned and he hooked one finger
where she'd tucked the edge of the towel to secure it.
One short tug and it lay on the carpet at her feet. His
sharp intake of air gave her courage.

"You're so beautiful," he said, skimming his fingertips over the swell of one breast. She trembled at his
touch, then caught her lower lip between her teeth.
Water dripped from his finger and slid down her breast
and over her nipple. His hand followed. Her eyes closed
as a surge of pleasure rocketed through her.

"I—I thought you didn't want me."

His touch was as light as a whisper as he made a path
over the curves and valleys of her breasts. He reached
for her hand and guided her to him. Her eyes flew open
when her fingertips met the satin-steel skin.

He chuckled softly. "Now tell me you think I don't
want you."

Just touching him excited her beyond reason. She'd
never felt like this with a man. He groaned when she
continued to explore the beauty of his body. "Make
love to me, Slade," she whispered.

He pulled her into the shower with him. When the
water struck Cassie's back, her eyes opened wide and
she shrieked.

Wrapping his arms around her, he lifted her and
turned her out of the spray. "I was taking a cold
shower."

She reached behind him and turned up the hot water, then slid her arms around his neck. "You don't need
one anymore," she breathed.

The tile was cool on Cassie's back as Slade pressed
her against the shower wall. Steam enveloped them like
a cocoon. His body was solid, smooth. Wet. She raised

her face to his, and when he kissed her, liquid fire swirled through her. His tongue sought hers and hungrily tasted, pleasured, then tasted again. His hands, slippery with soap, slid exquisitely over her body, kneading and caressing her skin, driving her crazy with delight.

Desire, as hot and piercing as the spray of water, shot through her. His muscles rippled and bunched beneath her wandering hands. He kissed her eyes, her chin, then lowered his head and kissed the beaded tip of her breast. She moaned as he took the peak into his mouth, then raked her hands through his wet hair and pulled him closer. She'd die if he couldn't get closer. His teeth were gentle, his tongue knowing, and when his hand moved between her thighs she bit her bottom lip to stop herself from crying out.

She wanted to beg him to hurry, but he seemed intent on taking his time. It was the sweetest, most painful torture she could have ever imagined. She bit the inside of her mouth and lay her head back against the tile. She gasped when his fingers slid inside her. Her nails dug into his back.

"Slade, please . . . I can't stand any more."

She did. He took her higher. Her hair lay wet against her face and shoulders. He stroked her, kissed her, teased her until she sobbed out his name.

With a groan, his mouth caught hers again. He lifted her, fitted her to him as she instinctively wrapped her legs around him. His strength held her securely. They moved together, slowly at first, then faster. He pressed his lips to her neck, called her name again and again.

Release, powerful and intense, flowed over them like a tidal wave. She muffled her cry against his shoulder; his pleasure thundered and echoed against the walls.

Together they slid to the floor.

Steam swirled around the bathroom in white, misty clouds. Cassie felt as if she were floating on one. She watched through heavy eyes as Slade rearranged the blanket of towels they'd carelessly tossed on the floor. When he stretched out beside her and tucked her body against his, she looped her arms around his neck.

"I don't think I can move," she whispered, nuzzling his chest.

"I know what you mean." His hands followed the curve of her spine then slipped down to cup her bottom. "Sight-seeing is exhausting."

"Hmm." Like a contented cat, Cassie snuggled closer.

Slowly, sensually, he rocked his hips against hers, and an ache spread low and hot through her, amazing her with its intensity. It was so soon, yet so right. She pressed her lips to his collarbone, tasted his damp skin. He groaned when she ran her teeth over his chest, then lightly bit his nipple.

She knew their time was running out; his plane would be leaving soon. Every minute, every second, was precious to her. If she couldn't tell him, she would show him how much she loved him. When he went back to Colorado, he'd have to know. And remember. She wanted him to remember always.

She explored his heated, damp skin with her hands, with her mouth. She stroked gently, persistently, until he clasped her head in his hands and dragged her mouth to his, then pulled her on top of him. He filled her senses, her heart, her body. They moved together and she clung to him, gasping as her climax arced. He grasped her hips tightly and thrust into her, then drew in a sharp, shuddering breath as he lost himself to her.

His arms came around her as she collapsed on his chest. Her heart beat frantically, matching the wild pounding of Slade's.

His breath was heavy as he nibbled on her ear. "What did you say about not being able to move?"

Exhausted, she laid her cheek against his neck. "I mean it this time."

Chuckling, he rolled to his side, bringing her with him. She lay like a rag doll in his arms. A sopping rag doll.

Slade kissed Cassie's closed eyes, and when she sighed he gathered her close to him. He needed to feel her against him, around him. Her face was flushed and damp, her hair shiny wet and dark against his chest. He cradled her head in his arm, watching her sleep, trying to ignore the pain that centered in his heart.

"Slade," she said softly, wearily.

"Hmm." He touched his lips to her shoulder.

"I have to go put your clothes in the dryer or you won't get out of here on time."

He stroked the lush curve of her breast. She was so soft, so sweet. "I'll wear them wet."

Sighing, she gently took his wrist and removed his hand. "You don't want to be late for your flight."

Anger, as inexplicable as it was irrational, wound its way through him. Releasing her, he sat up and dragged a hand through his dripping hair. "No, we wouldn't want that now, would we?"

He quickly averted his gaze when she looked at him strangely. He hadn't intended his words to sound so cold, but his body was still ablaze from the feel and taste of her, and he felt as if she were shoving him out the

door. Though it should have relieved him, it made him
mad as hell she was taking his leaving with such aplomb.

"There's a comb in the drawer by the sink," she said,
wrapping a towel around her. She planted a brief kiss on
his cheek and rose. "I'll take care of your clothes and
get dressed. That should still give us plenty of time to
get you to the airport for your flight."

"Great," he muttered, admiring her bare legs as she
walked out of the bathroom. Long, shapely legs that
only a few minutes ago had been wrapped around him.
Desire bolted through him once again. He reined it in,
then forced it from his mind. There was no time for
those thoughts.

He had a flight to catch.

An hour later, on the way to the airport, Slade noted
the time on the dashboard clock of Cassie's compact.
Five-fifty. His plane left at 6:30.

The freeway was jammed; horns blared; motorists
made crude gestures to each other; cars cut sharply in
and out of traffic. He knew it was going to be close.

A deep vibration shook Cassie's car, and it took Slade
a moment to realize the source was the radio of the
small truck beside them. Carnegie Hall would be proud
of those speakers, he thought irritably.

Beside him, seemingly unconcerned, Cassie tapped
her fingers to a song on the radio. Anxious, he
drummed his fingers on his thigh.

"Are we going to make it?" he asked.

"Of course we are." She smiled at him.

When they finally entered the airport parking lot,
Slade watched his plane take off.

While Cassie parked the car, Slade went inside the
airport. She met him at the ticket counter. "Were you
able to get another flight?"

He shook his head. "Not confirmed until Sunday morning. All the other flights are booked until then." He sighed and scanned the waiting area in the terminal. "I can always get a hotel, or dig in here and go standby."

"You have another option." Cassie took a slow, deep breath and slipped the thin leather strap of her purse farther up her shoulder. Slade looked at her. She met his steady gaze. "You can stay with me."

Indecision haunted his eyes. Sighing, he glanced away, then back again. "Cassie, I—"

"What's the matter?" She forced a smile. "Is the thought of life in the city for two days more than you can handle?"

He considered wiping that sassy tone out of her voice with a kiss. Instead he folded his arms and lifted his brows. "Is that a challenge?"

"A survival weekend in the city, Slade. Think you can cut the mustard?"

He doubted it. But it had nothing to do with the city, and everything to do with Cassie. "I'm sure you've already made plans," he offered. "I'd just be in the way."

She nodded. "I do have a clambake to attend at a client's cottage out on Cape Cod, but parties are part of the itinerary of a survival weekend."

He laughed. "I didn't bring anything with me."

She grinned up at him. "What was it you said to me in the mountains, something about sharing? What I don't have we can pick up at the store."

His smile slowly faded. "Cassie, you know why I shouldn't stay."

"For God's sake," she said, exasperated, "all I'm offering is a place to sleep. I even have a second bedroom that locks if it scares you so bad to be alone with me.''

It scared the hell out of him. Every minute he stayed with her made it more difficult for him to leave. He glanced quickly around the noisy, crowded terminal. Did he want to spend his weekend here, trying to sleep on a hard plastic chair, or go home with Cassie and be with her?

He might be a fool, but he wasn't a stupid fool.

He grinned down at her. ''Tell me,'' he said taking her by the arm and leading her to the parking lot, ''is the lock on the bedroom on the outside or the inside?''

Ten

Somewhere a dog was barking. Slade opened his eyes, but the blast of sunlight he encountered forced them closed again. Cassie snuggled deeper into the crook of his arm and crossed one long shapely leg over his. He was awake instantly.

Cassie's bed was like a giant pillow. He sank down in the soft mattress, pulling her closer to him. Making love to her in a bed was every bit as enjoyable as the shower and forest. He kissed the top of her head and surrendered to the feel of her warm, soft skin against his. Her body fitted to his perfectly. He marveled at that. That and the fact that he couldn't get enough of her. He would be content to lie here the entire day with her curled against him like this.

He could lie here a lifetime.

Frowning, he pushed that thought down. He had less than twenty-four hours. Twenty-four hours to store up every smile, every gesture, the sound of her voice, the feel of her skin. He ran his fingers over one shoulder now, watched her cuddle closer to him. There was so much he wanted to take home with him, to remember. Winters in the Rockies were long and cold.

Suddenly, in the condo next door, a man's voice boomed out an exaggerated rendition of Frank Sinatra's "My Way." Slade gritted his teeth and rolled his eyes, then looked down at her slumbering, peaceful form. Her hair, a dark mass of tangled curls, fanned out across her pillow. Her face was pale and delicate, her lips rosy and inviting. He cupped her rounded bare bottom with one hand, then let his fingers drift lazily up her spine. She murmured sleepily and arched her body against his. He held on to her to steady himself, imagining what an eagle must feel like as it swooped down to the earth then soared heaven-bound again.

With his free hand, he skimmed the curve of her hip, then over her stomach...

Two blasts from a horn directly outside the window jerked him upright. Startled by his sudden movement, Cassie clung to him and gasped, "What's the matter?"

"You honestly didn't hear that?" He tossed the covers back and threw one leg over the side of the bed.

"Where are you going?"

"To tell that idiot to shut up."

"Oh no you don't." She grabbed him. "That's Mr. Myers picking up Mrs. Anderson for their Saturday-morning craft class. She's seventy and he's seventy-two. It's too difficult for him to climb the stairs and get her, so he always honks."

Mollified, Slade slid back between the covers and pulled her against him. He nuzzled her neck, kissed that sensitive spot behind her ear he'd discovered last night.

She moaned and wrapped her arms around him, whispering his name, arousing him with her touch. He could get used to this . . . Cassie cuddled beside him every morning, every night.

What he couldn't get used to was that damn fool singing next door.

Exasperated, he sat up.

"Now what's the matter?" She gazed up at him through sleepy eyes.

"How can you sleep through all this racket?"

"The only thing bothering my sleep is you jumping up and down," she said, sighing. She leaned forward and slid her arms around his waist. His bare back was warm against her body, and she felt her breasts tighten at the contact. She buried her face in the back of his neck and kissed him.

He twisted around and drew her down onto the bed with him. His lips moved over her neck, down to her breast . . . then he raised his head and stilled.

"Do you own a dog?"

"No," she gasped, dragging his lips down to hers.

He kissed her long and hard, then pulled away again. "I hear a dog—in your living room."

She sighed and wiggled out from under him. "That's my neighbor's dog across the hall." She stood and pulled on a short silky robe. "They're just out for their morning walk."

"Oh." He reached for her, but she grabbed his wrist and held it. Frowning, she sat back down on the edge of the bed.

"Slade," she said hesitantly, "I sort of have a confession."

Not liking the tone in her voice one bit, he sat up carefully. "What's that?"

"Uh, yesterday, on the way to the airport..."

"Yes?"

"Well, I sort of...took the long way."

He raised his brows. "The long way?"

She cleared her throat. "Yes, well, the way I took you I knew we'd never make it there on time."

He stared at her, letting her words sink in. "So what you're telling me is that you intentionally made me miss my plane."

She drew in a slow breath and stood. "Yes."

When he still said nothing, she asked, "Are you mad?"

"Mad?" he repeated, throwing the covers off. "Why would I be mad?" He started off the bed, his movements as calculated and precise as a cat creeping toward a bird.

The devilish glint of mischief in his eyes told Cassie he wasn't truly mad, but retribution was close at hand. She backed toward the door. "Let's talk about this over coffee, shall we?" She reached for the doorknob. "I'll go put it on."

When she dashed out, he sat on the edge of the bed, trying to absorb what she'd just admitted to him. She'd actually gone to all this trouble so he'd stay? How could he possibly be mad? He started to laugh. Isn't that what he'd done to her in the mountains? Wasn't that the real reason he'd dragged her around for two days, because he'd wanted to be with her?

Lying back, he turned his face into Cassie's pillow and breathed in her feminine scent. The bed was cold without her. Lonely. She wasn't even gone two minutes and he missed her already.

He would be home right now if he hadn't missed his flight. And he would have missed the most incredible night of his life. After they'd left the airport, they stopped to pick up some toiletries for him, then come back to Cassie's condo. They'd intended to go out again for dinner, but somehow they'd ended up in bed. Somehow hell. He sat up and dragged his jeans on. Both of them knew that's where they'd end up, where they wanted to be.

Smiling, he ventured out of the bedroom and headed for the kitchen. He could hear that damn dog barking right outside the front door. Without thinking, he pulled it open.

He met the startled face of Cassie's neighbor. She stood in the hall, a paper in one hand, a leash in her other. A fluffy little dog with no face yipped all the louder at Slade's appearance. The woman stared at Slade's bare chest and her mouth fell open. Scowling, he slammed the door again.

"Was someone at the door?" Cassie called out from the kitchen.

"One of your neighbors."

She walked into the living room, a can of coffee still in her hand. "What did they want?"

He shrugged. "I haven't a clue."

She glanced to the door, then back at Slade. Sighing, she shook her head. "Have you always been such a misanthrope?"

He grabbed his chest as if she'd speared him. "Me? A misanthrope? I love people." He moved toward her, his expression feigned hurt. He removed the coffee from her hands, set it on an end table, then pulled her into his arms. "It's just neighbors I can't stand. Specifically—" he lowered his mouth to hers "—*your* neighbors."

When his lips brushed hers, the last thing on Cassie's mind was her neighbors. Fingers spread, she placed her palms on his chest, felt the rough texture of his hair, the fierce pounding of his heart.

"What time is that party today?" he whispered, pressing feather-light kisses on the corners of her mouth.

"Hmm?" His fingers were doing something erotically magical to her spine.

"The clambake," he murmured. "You know, the one you can't miss at the cottage."

"Oh, that party." His touch sent sparks racing over her skin. She had to think hard to come up with an answer. "Two o'clock." Somewhere between a sigh and a moan she ran her hands over the hard planes and angles of his chest and shoulders. She was awed by the power she felt emanate from his taut body.

"Then, to repeat a phrase I heard somewhere, I suggest we make the most of the time we have." He slipped his hands around her waist and tucked her intimately against him.

She answered him by sliding her arms around his neck and pulling him closer. She deepened the kiss, moving her tongue hungrily against his. She felt, rather than heard, the low rumble of a moan in his throat. His arms tightened around her, molded her to him.

Wave after wave of sensation swept over her. Her nipples rubbed against the silk fabric of her robe, then against warm skin as he tugged the obstructing garment out of the way. Pleasure spilled through her at the contact. No man had ever made her feel like this before, so free, so uninhibited. She knew, without a doubt, no man ever would again. She realized he was not ready to hear the words, but she needed him to know—to feel—how much she loved him.

Her robe floated to the floor. His breathing was erratic as he murmured her name, his hands skillful and gentle as they skimmed over her breasts. She moaned, digging her fingers into his hair, suddenly afraid he might let go. "Hold me," she whispered.

They held each other, moving toward the bedroom, all the while touching, tasting, with a fervor that left them both breathless. It was as if they were back in the mountains, with the storm circling them. Only now the storm was inside her, crashing and thundering, racing through her blood, pounding in her ears. He laid her on the bed, his eyes dark as pewter as he covered her body with his. She sank down in the mattress, pulling him with her. Together they rode the storm.

The cottage turned out to be a three-story, thirty-two-room mansion on Cape Cod. A rainbow of party balloons decorated food-laden tables, soft music from a three-piece combo drifted on the afternoon sea breeze, and the murmur of a "small" gathering—somewhere around a hundred twenty-five or fifty wealthy guests—mingled in groups on the huge redwood deck overlooking the Cape.

Polo shirts and deck shoes were the official party uniform. Slade glanced down at his own attire—blue shirt and jeans. Talk about a square peg in a round hole.

Slade decided he loved parties about as much as Cassie loved bats.

"Hi." Cassie appeared and handed him a glass of champagne. "How you holding up?"

Sunlight sparkled off her hair; her eyes, the color of warm brandy, smiled at him, touched him like only a lover's could. His throat went dry as he stared at her. He had the craziest notion to kidnap her. Just pack a bag and drag her off to Colorado. Take the chance that just maybe she wouldn't grow bored with the solitude...with him. The roar of the ocean and the clinking of champagne glasses brought him back to reality. Her reality.

"I said—" she leaned closer "—how are you doing?"

"Terrific. I'm having a great time." Her perfume was light and flowery. He wanted to wrap himself around her and show her exactly "how he was doing." He downed half of the champagne she'd given him. "Is it time to go yet?"

She laughed. "Well, let's see," she said, glancing at her watch, "we've been here four minutes, so maybe in another three or four we can sneak off." Her eyes scanned the guests. "I do have to stay at least until my father gets here. Our host, Charles Overby, is one of my father's wealthiest clients. Phillips, Weston and Roe has to be represented."

The thought of seeing Cassie's father would not normally brighten Slade's day, but considering it meant he could be alone with Cassie, Slade suddenly couldn't wait for the man to appear. For the moment, though, he would have to be satisfied with the pleasure of looking. The breeze caught the hem of the navy polka-dot dress she wore and swirled it around her shapely calves. She looked perfectly at home here among the rich, her hair loose and flowing in an ocean breeze, her smile warm and generous to everyone who passed by. It was obvious she enjoyed this life. His fingers tightened around the fragile stem of the champagne glass and he downed the remaining liquid.

"Cassie!"

Cassie turned and saw Jackie wave from the French doors leading to the patio. Her heart sank. She didn't relish the thought of sharing what little time she had left with Slade. Especially with Jackie. She had built-in radar for single men, and though Cassie knew Jackie couldn't help it, there were times—like now—that it was exasperating.

"Hi, Cassie." Jackie's eyes were on Slade. "And hello again to you, Mr. Mason."

"Please, call me Slade."

Did he have to smile like that at the woman? Cassie thought irritably. And did Jackie have to look at Slade as if she'd never seen a man before? Cassie plastered a smile to her lips, thinking her face might break any minute. Jackie was busy chattering on about how much she loved Colorado and just what exactly did he do there anyway? She squealed when Slade told her he was a professor. Of course, she encouraged, he just *had* to tell her all about it.

When Jackie touched Slade's arm and laughed, Cassie decided she'd had enough. Prepared to drag the man off if necessary, she started to step forward. A hand on her elbow stopped her. Cassie groaned silently when she saw who it was.

"Cassandra, how good to see you."

"It's lovely to see you, too, Jared." She moved to kiss him on the cheek, but he turned his face and their lips brushed. She managed a smile, despite the fact her jaw was clenched.

Jared looked as if he'd just stepped off his yacht. His tan was fresh, his brown hair streaked blond. His smile was brilliantly white and incredibly phony, but Jackie, who was standing between the two gorgeous men, looked as if she'd died and gone to heaven.

"Jared, this is Slade Mason." She turned to Slade and noticed his eyes had darkened to the color of gunpowder. "Slade, this is Jared Overby, our host's son."

The men shook hands cordially, but Cassie sensed a wariness between them.

"You look familiar," Jared said. "Have I seen you at the club?"

"I doubt it." Slade shook his head.

"Slade is from Colorado," Cassie explained.

"Ah." He looked Slade over. "Are you here on business?"

"Personal."

Cassie felt her heart pick up speed when Slade looked over at her. His gaze burned through her, and she felt her cheeks color and her toes curl at the same time.

Squaring her shoulders, Cassie tore her attention from Slade. "Jackie, what time is my father supposed to get here?"

"Didn't you know?" Jackie appeared genuinely surprised. "Your father couldn't make it. He had a last-minute meeting to attend."

That's just great, Cassie fumed silently. She'd have to stay longer if her father wasn't here. Whether she liked it or not, these affairs were part of her job. And right now she definitely did not like it.

"I was just telling Father it's been too long since you came out and played tennis," Jared was saying to her. "We insist you come on Sunday."

"Well, I—I'm not sure I—"

"You can bring Mr. Mason along with you." Realizing Jackie was still standing there, Jared's good manners took over. "And of course, you're welcome, too."

Jackie beamed. Slade frowned. Cassie wanted to scream.

"Thanks for the offer," Slade said coolly, "but I'll be catching a plane."

"Well then, there's no reason Cassie can't come by." Jared smiled at her. "We'll have brunch after we play." He took Cassie's hand. "Mr. Mason, Jackie, if you could excuse us for a moment, I must have a private word with Cassandra here regarding a business matter. I promise to return her safe and sound in just a few."

Slade's narrowed eyes met Cassie's apologetic ones. She saw him flex his jaw as Jared took her arm and led her away. Blast it, anyway! She'd brought him here hoping to spend some time with him while she did her duty to her father's company. The temptation to simply walk away and worry about facing Martin Phillips's wrath later was tremendous. She glanced back at Slade, who was watching her, his expression cold as stone. She started to turn back when her host, Jared's father, approached. There was no way out now. She was caught, and she'd just have to suffer through it. She turned away and smiled at Charles Overby, thanked him for inviting her, then felt herself pulled farther away from Slade.

Later, she told herself. She'd make it up to him later.

Slade was beginning to think he just might not survive this weekend after all.

He nodded politely as an attractive blonde on his right related every excruciating detail of her trip to Colorado last year. The back of his head ached from forcing polite smiles. His face felt freeze-dried. The lady's husband, to Slade's left, had just finished a rather lengthy explanation on the downward trend of the current market and then leaned in close when he offered Slade an inside tip on a stock.

His ears were numb. Hell, his *brain* was numb.

Excusing himself from the fascinating couple, Slade moved through the crowd, searching for Cassie. Pretty-boy Jared had been stuck to her all afternoon like a gnat on a lollipop. Slade stopped at the edge of the deck, and when he couldn't find either one of them he felt his stomach tighten and his jaw clench.

He'd had enough of parties and people. He started to turn, determined to get the hell out of this place he didn't belong or want to be.

That's when he saw her. Standing on the beach, by herself. Her sandals lay in the sand beside her bare feet, her hands were clasped behind her back. She lifted her face to the late-afternoon sun, and her hair caught in the breeze like a brilliant silky mane. The ocean breeze kicked up her skirt and showed her long, shapely legs.

He forgot to breathe. He'd never seen her more beautiful. His throat constricted as he watched her, and pain filled his chest.

He knew at that instant, without a doubt, that he loved her. That he would always love her.

If you really love someone you have to let them go. That's what he'd told Cassie when they'd first met. He'd been speaking of Sarah, of course. But his words came back to haunt him now and he knew they were true. He watched a sea gull swoop down close to her and land a few feet away. Her smile lighted her face, the beach.

He loved her.

And he would have to let her go.

Cassie turned when she sensed someone approach. When she saw it was Slade, her smile widened, then slowly died. The look on his face frightened her. She'd known they were going to have to talk before the weekend was over, but it was too soon. Too soon. He stopped in front of her and her eyes met his.

"I was just coming up to the house," she said, forcing a smile.

"It's time for me to go, Cassie."

She started to move. "I'll just say my goodbyes and—"

His hand stopped her. "I'm not going back with you."

Hurt sliced through her. She bit the inside of her mouth so she could feel something other than the horrible pain in her heart. She looked away from him. "Why?"

"It won't work between us," he said softly. "It might for a while, but this is where you belong."

Damn this man's stubbornness! She lifted her chin. "And you're qualified to make that decision for me, of course."

"Yes." He looked away from her, out across the ocean.

Anger whipped through her. It felt so much better than the pain. "You're a hypocrite, Slade Mason," she said, her feet planted firmly in the sand. "You're great at giving advice, but lousy at taking it."

He looked back at her. "What are you talking about?"

"When I came to Colorado, determined to bring Sarah home, you told me no one has the right to make another person's decisions for them."

His eyes narrowed. "That was different."

"Really?" She folded her arms. "How?"

Frustrated, he raked a hand through his hair and swore. "Cassie, I've been there before. I've seen what it does to a woman to be cooped up in the mountains. You said it yourself when you first showed up at my cabin—the isolation would make you crazy. You'd end up hating me." He let out a long, weary breath. "That's not a chance I'm willing to take."

"A chance *you're* willing to take?" She stepped closer and lifted her face to his. "You listen to me and listen well, mister. I'm not your ex-wife. I don't give a damn what kind of life you had together. It has *nothing* to do with you and me."

"It's not just the way I live, Cassie." He swept a hand toward the mansion, the beach. "There're no parties or yachts with me. Boredom will set in quickly after the first snow."

For the first time in her life she wanted to strike someone. White-hot fury rocketed through her. She balled her fists at her sides, restraining the urge to swing at him.

"This is part of my life, Slade," she said, her voice barely controlled. "I don't have to defend that to you. But you're a fool if you think any of this is more important to me than us."

She spun away from him, took a deep breath of ocean air, then faced him again. "You know what you need, Slade?" She poked him in the chest with her index finger. "You need a good strong dose of trust. I'm tired of trying to convince you we have something special, something worth taking that risk you're so damned afraid of. If you're too pigheaded to realize that yourself, then just go on back to Colorado."

She moved close to him, lifted her face to his. "Just do this for me, Slade. Whenever there's a thunderstorm, remember the feel of my lips and my skin. Every time you walk through that damn forest, remember the first time you made love to me on the grass. Every time you take a shower, remember me in your arms." She stepped away from him, her eyes burning with tears. "Remember me, Slade, because that's all you're going to have—memories."

She snatched up her sandals and walked away from him, toward the house, back to the party.

Out of his life.

Eleven

It was the perfect day for a wedding.

The Rocky Mountain sky was blue as a robin's egg, the air clean and fresh and laden with the sharp scent of pine. Cougar Pass anxiously awaited the marriage of Mason and Sarah. Since the entire town was invited, the streets were empty as Slade drove down the main street and parked his truck in front of town hall. White and pink ribbons and balloons formed a huge arch over the hall's double entry doors. Streamers draped across the front of the building waved in the morning breeze.

Picture-perfect, Slade thought as he cut the engine of his truck. He was happy for Sarah and Mason. They had each other. The coming baby. Years to grow up and grow old, to laugh and fight and love.

Longing rose in his chest. He thought of Cassie. His palms grew damp as he realized she was probably already in the hall, waiting. But not for him. Seven days ago she'd walked out of his life, making it clear the next move was his. He'd almost made that move, too. About a hundred times. On the way to the airport he nearly had the driver turn around, at the airport he stopped himself a dozen times from heading straight back to her place. All week long he'd wanted to call her, hear her voice.

Tell her he loved her.

He'd thought about what she said to him on the beach. That he had no right to make decisions for her. No matter how he looked at it, he knew she was right. He realized he hadn't just been protecting Cassie from an unsuccessful relationship, he had been protecting himself. She was also right when she'd said he was afraid to take a risk. The thought of being with her, really being with her, then having her leave, was more than he could bear. He didn't just want to live with Cassie.

He wanted to marry her.

That realization had hit him somewhere around Tuesday. He hadn't had a sane thought since. He drew in a deep breath, opened the truck's door and stepped out. He walked toward the hall, thinking he might never have a sane thought again.

Cassie closed the top pearl button at the back of her sister's satin-and-lace gown, readjusted a loose strand of baby's breath in her upswept hair, then turned her around and stepped back. Sarah's cheeks were flushed, her lips brushed with pink, her blue eyes glowing with happiness. Cassie's chest constricted as she looked at her sister. Tears filled her eyes.

"Oh no you don't." Sarah pointed a warning finger. "You promised me you wouldn't cry. If you cry, then I'm going to have to cry and—" With a groan, Sarah turned and rushed over to the makeup table. She snatched up a tissue, sat down, then dabbed at her eyes. "You've done it now, Cass. I'm going to walk out there looking like a raccoon."

Cassie walked behind Sarah and looked at her reflection in the mirror. "You're going to walk out there and be the most beautiful bride in the world." She reached down and hugged her. "Mom would have been so happy."

They said nothing for a moment, just held each other. Sniffling, Sarah finally pulled away. "You look pretty gorgeous yourself. That dress is a knockout on you. Pink is definitely your color."

"It might be your color pretty soon, too," Cassie teased.

Sarah beamed. "Pink or blue, I'm happy either way."

Cassie looked at her sister. "When are you going to tell Dad?"

Sighing, Sarah met Cassie's gaze. "Mason wanted to tell him as soon as you both came in yesterday, but you got here so late I didn't think it would be a good idea."

"Sorry." Cassie smiled apologetically. "I was driving and took a wrong turn."

"It was fine with me." Sarah reached for her eyeliner and touched up her eyes. "My suggestion was we slip him a note as we're driving off on our honeymoon." She grinned. "We compromised. We're going to tell him during the reception." She set down the makeup and faced Cassie. "I was hoping you'd be there with us."

Cassie took her sister's hand and squeezed it. "I'd love to."

"Speaking of telling people things." Sarah turned back to the mirror. "When are you going to tell Slade how you feel about him?"

Dumbstruck, Cassie stared at her sister. "What?"

Sarah swept a fresh coat of lipstick on her mouth. "Slade. You know, Mason's best man. When are you going to tell him you love him?"

The words to deny it were on the tip of her tongue. But this was Sarah she was talking to. There was no way she could lie. However, she wasn't quite ready to admit it yet, either. "Why would I tell him I love him?"

"Well, for one thing," Sarah said, tucking a loose curl back where it belonged, "to put the poor man out of his misery. And for another thing, because you do. Love him, I mean."

Afraid that Sarah would see her hand shaking, Cassie clutched the tissue and dabbed at her eyes. "I don't know what you're talking about. Slade's not in any misery because of me."

"Oh, right." Sarah laughed. "That's why he spent the last four mornings hanging around our cabin like a starving hound looking for a bone. If he asked me one question about you, he asked a hundred." She shook her head, grinning. "Oh, he tried to be subtle, as if he's asking polite questions about me, but he always comes back around to the subject of you."

Cassie's heart was pounding so hard she had to take in a slow breath to calm herself. "What kind of questions?"

"It would be easier to tell you what he *didn't* ask," she replied. "Everything from the kind of music you like to the type of food you eat."

That was the craziest thing she'd ever heard. "Watch out the squirrels don't get you, Sis. You've gone nuts."

Sarah shrugged. "All I know is I never heard more than a few words out of Slade all the time I've been up here. These last few days, he never stopped."

Slade? Sarah had to be talking about some other man. "Why would he ask questions about me?"

Sarah rolled her eyes and sighed. "You're the older one here who's supposed to know all these things. For God's sake, Cassie, the man loves you."

Cassie closed her eyes and let the hurt roll through her. "That's where you're wrong," she said quietly. "I threw myself at the man and he still turned me away."

"Cassie—"

She felt the tears well up and raised a hand, cutting Sarah off. "Enough. This is your wedding day and we're going to think nothing but happy thoughts. I'll deal with my own problems later."

Sighing, Sarah nodded. "Okay, Cass. Whatever you say. Just remember, Slade loves you, whether he wants to admit it or not. And you love him. It doesn't have to be any more complicated than that unless you let it."

From the hall, the strains of the organ floated to them, and they both turned their heads, listening.

"It's time," Sarah whispered, her eyes wide.

Cassie moved toward the door. "I'll go tell them you're ready."

When she stepped into the hall, Cassie hesitated, reflecting on Sarah's words and wondering when her baby sister had gotten so old and so wise. She stared at the door, then down the hallway where the guests waited.

Where Slade waited.

A smile crept slowly over her lips as the wedding march began.

It was time.

Slade knew he should be watching the bride, but the minute Cassie appeared, everything around him—Mason, the guests, the organist—all of it melted away, leaving only her.

She was stunning. A breathtaking vision in pink lace and pearls. Her smile was radiant, her eyes sparkling. She'd pulled her hair into a knot at the back of her head and sprinkled tiny white and pink flowers there. Dozens of loose curls cascaded around her glowing face. He had to stop himself from stepping toward her.

No more than two feet away, she turned her gaze to him before she moved to take her place. Her smile widened, her eyes touched him, and for that one brief moment he felt the first flicker of hope. At best, he'd expected a cool reception from her.

Perhaps her unpredictability was part of the reason he loved her so much.

He tried to listen to the minister's words, to Mason and Sarah's vows. He really did. But his thoughts, his eyes, continually drifted to her. He kept imagining this scenario with the players shuffled around. Himself for Mason, Cassie for Sarah. He thought of this past week, of every minute he'd been without her. He did not want her to walk out of his life one more time.

His fear of losing her later had finally succumbed to his fear of never having her at all.

Music blasted from the organ, and they were walking back down the aisle, together, her hand lightly tucked in the crook of his arm. She smelled like flowers and sunshine. They reached the end of the aisle and he started to pull her away where they could be alone. A photographer intervened and five seconds later she was gone, mixing with the guests, smiling, laughing.

It was a long time later, after the food, the champagne, when she was on her second dance—a slow one—with Tom Miller, the owner of Cougar Pass Hay and Feed, that he'd decided he'd waited long enough. Tom reluctantly stepped away when Slade cut in.

"Hello, Slade." She placed her hand on his shoulder and smiled up at him.

Hello? How could she stand here so calmly in his arms, smile so politely, and just say hello? He'd been twisted up in knots for the past week just thinking about her, and she was treating him like one of her father's clients.

Okay, he reasoned, maybe he didn't deserve a warm welcome. He knew he had hurt her. She just needed a little time to come around. "You look beautiful, Cassie."

"Thanks. You look great, too."

She was looking over his shoulder, past the other couples dancing. He turned to follow the direction of her gaze. Sarah was standing in the corner, Mason beside her, his head bowed as he listened to her.

"Cassie," Slade said impatiently, and she turned her attention back to him. "Cassie—" his voice came a little softer "—I'm trying to tell you I'm sorry."

He felt a slight stiffening of her body, then she relaxed again. "Sorry about what?"

The music switched to a fast beat. Swearing, he grabbed her wrist and pulled her through the other dancers to the side of the room. He sucked in a breath, then quickly said, "I'm sorry I've been such a jerk."

She leaned up and brushed her cheek against his. "It's okay."

Frustration had him grabbing her shoulders. "What do you mean, 'it's okay?'"

"Slade—" she laughed "—what do you want me to say?"

He stuck his hands in his pockets and frowned. Damn if she wasn't making this difficult. And why was she looking over his shoulder again? Irritated, he glanced behind him and noticed that Cassie's father had joined Sarah and Mason.

"Cassie, I—"

"Slade," she interrupted him, touching his arm, "could we please finish this discussion later? I have to give Sarah a hand with something."

She turned away so abruptly he didn't have a chance to answer. Finish this discussion later? That was a brush-off if he'd ever heard one, he thought angrily. His hands twisted into fists, and he had the insane urge to punch a hole in the wall. Instead he folded his arms and stood there, watching her walk away and join her family. When they left the reception hall and moved into the privacy of the outer corridor, a low, dull ache settled deep in his chest.

Slade jammed the truck's gearshift into third and roared up the dusty mountain road toward his cabin. Clouds of dust blocked out his rearview mirror, and the sound of flying rocks buffeted the underside of the truck.

She hadn't even said goodbye.

How could she leave like that? he thought, down-shifting and braking to negotiate a sharp turn. He'd stood around waiting for her like an overanxious teen-ager, ready to tell her he loved her, that he wanted to marry her, only to find out from Mason that she'd left the reception and wasn't coming back.

A fresh wave of hurt coursed through him. She was the best thing that ever happened to him and he'd let her slip through his fingers. Anger took the place of hurt, and he cursed himself for being such a fool.

A pine branch slapped against his windshield when he drove too close to the edge of the road. He knew he was going too fast, he just didn't care. When the truck hit a pothole the impact threw his head against the roof of the cab, then jerked him forward. There was a loud bang, the bed of the truck fishtailed then bounced to a stop.

With a curse, he flung open the door and stepped into the dust cloud now enveloping his truck. Coughing, he stormed to the front of the pickup. Dammit! The right front tire had blown. He knelt down to inspect it then swore some more. The rim was bent, too.

"Great, just great," he said loudly, resisting the urge to punch the fender. He looked down at his white dress shirt and suit slacks. Changing the tire required climbing under the truck and pulling out the spare. His clothes would never survive.

He'd have to walk to the cabin, change clothes, then come back. A squirrel twitched his tail, and chattered at him from the low branch of an aspen. Slade scowled at the irritating creature, then set off, muttering a few choice words.

He hadn't gone more than a few feet when he noticed his No Trespassing sign. He stopped and stared at it for a moment, then marched over and gave it a good kick, knocking it over.

He'd be damned if he'd let Cassie Phillips get away from him. If he had to go to Boston and make her listen to him, then that's what he'd do. She was going to marry him and that's all there was to it. He gave a snort of sarcastic laughter. As if anything that had to do with Cassie could be that simple.

Every step of the way reminded Slade he was coming home to an empty house. By the time he stomped up his front steps he was covered with dust, his head hurt where he'd hit it on the roof of the cab, and somehow he'd picked up a pebble in his sock.

He threw open the front door and slammed it shut. He started for the bedroom, then froze.

Dressed in jeans and a blue chambray shirt, Cassie was sitting at the kitchen table. She had a map spread out in front of her and she appeared to be engrossed in it. He simply stared at her, afraid she might disappear if he spoke. She looked up at him.

"Oh, hi, Slade. I was hoping you'd get here so you could help me with this."

He wanted to run to her and pull her into his arms, but his feet refused to move. He'd been so sure she'd gone back to Boston. That she'd left him. "Help you?" he finally managed.

"Yes." She looked back at the map. "I just can't seem to figure this out."

Tentatively he moved closer. "I thought you'd gone back to Boston."

"That's part of the problem," she said, tapping her finger on the map. "I was going to, but I got lost."

He stood beside her, breathing in the lingering scent of flowers she'd worn in her hair that morning. "Lost?"

"Well, I thought I was until I took a closer look at this map."

He glanced over her shoulder at the map. There was a red circle where his cabin would be, and several inked-in roads. All of them leading to Cougar Pass.

"I finally figured out this was the right road, though." She pointed to the one leading to his cabin, then looked up at him. "Actually," she said, meeting his intense gaze with her own, "it's the only road."

He reached for her wrist, closing his eyes as he hauled her out of the chair to him. She laid her cheek against his chest, and he gently wrapped one arm around her, afraid he might hurt her if he let himself go and hugged her the way he wanted to. He held her like that for a moment, whispering her name, brushing the top of her hair with his lips.

"I've been such a fool," he said.

"Uh-huh."

"I was trying to apologize to you at the wedding before you left."

She snuggled deeper in his arms. "I told you we'd finish the discussion later, didn't I?"

"That reminds me," he said, lifting her chin with his index finger. He stared down at her. "Why did you leave like that?"

"I had to see my father's face when Sarah told him he was going to be a grandfather." She smiled. "After she did, I couldn't tell from the look on his face whether he was going to punch Mason in the face or kiss him."

"And?"

She laughed. "He kissed Sarah and hugged Mason, then lit into me for not telling him." Cassie smiled up at Slade. "A son-in-law he actually likes and an upcoming grandbaby. I don't think I've ever seen him so happy."

"How would you like to make him twice as happy?"

Confused, she simply stared at him.

"I want you to marry me, Cassie."

Stunned, she leaned back and looked into Slade's face. "Have you thought about this?"

He laughed, startling her. "Only a couple of hundred times in the last week." He drew her back into his arms. "Every time I walked outside, looked at a pine tree, and especially—" his lips brushed hers "—every time I took a shower."

She deepened the kiss and snuggled closer. He smelled like dust and sweat and Slade. Feelings overwhelmed her and she clung to him, needing to steady herself. "You mean something I said to you actually penetrated that thick skull of yours?"

He tightened his arms around her. "I may be slow to grasp some things," he said, "but once I catch hold, I never let go."

She pressed her lips to his neck and whispered, "I hope that's me you're talking about."

"That's exactly who I'm talking about. I love you, Cass. The idea of living here without you, living anywhere without you, is inconceivable."

"You aren't going to lose me, Slade." Cassie slid her arms around his neck. "And the only place I want to live is here, with you."

He held her, kissed her temple, her cheek. When he brought her hand up to his lips, he stopped suddenly. "You aren't wearing a watch."

"Why would I need a watch in the mountains? We'll get up with the sun and go to bed with the dark." She brushed his lips with hers. "Or maybe sooner."

He pulled her against him. They'd never get out of bed if he had his way. "I only have a year left on the grant," he said tentatively. "We can always get a place in Denver if—"

Frowning, she stopped him with a kiss. "Slade, listen to me and listen well. I love it up here. If I start feeling cooped up, I can visit Sarah, not to mention my soon-to-be niece or nephew. And Denver isn't that far away, for heaven's sake."

He wanted her to be sure. Really sure. "And what about your job?"

She smiled. "I decided that even if you didn't want me it was time for a change in my life. I already told my father he was going to have to find a new director of Human Resources." She looked up at him. "I was thinking about social work. A few classes at the university will give me the credits I need."

He couldn't stop the twinge of doubt. "I have to warn you. The winters here are cold and long. Occasionally I'm gone for days at a time, and I'm rarely on time for anything."

She frowned at him. "If you're trying to back out of marrying me, Slade, you're in for a fight."

He laughed and pulled her closer, kissing her neck. "I love you, Cassie."

"And I love you." She slipped her arms around his neck. "I find the prospect of spending cold, long winters with you extremely arousing."

Reaching up, she kissed him, molding her body to his. He wrapped his arms tightly around her, drawing her even closer, deepening the kiss until they were both breathless.

She pulled away, gasping. "Slade," she said, unbuttoning his dusty shirt, "I think we need to take a shower."

* * * * *

From the popular author of the bestselling title
DUNCAN'S BRIDE (Intimate Moments #349)
comes the

LINDA
HOWARD
COLLECTION

Two exquisite collector's editions that contain four of
Linda Howard's early passionate love stories. To add
these special volumes to your own library, be sure
to look for:

VOLUME ONE: *Midnight Rainbow*
Diamond Bay
(Available in March)

VOLUME TWO: *Heartbreaker*
White Lies
(Available in April)

 *Silhouette Books*®

SLH92

The Case of the Mesmerizing Boss
DIANA PALMER

Diana Palmer's exciting new series,
MOST WANTED, begins in March with
THE CASE OF THE MESMERIZING BOSS....

Dane Lassiter—one-time Texas Ranger
extraordinaire—now heads his own group of
crack private detectives. Soul-scarred by
women, this heart-stopping private eyeful
exists only for his work—until the night his
secretary, Tess Meriwether, becomes the target
of drug dealers. Dane wants to keep her safe.
But their stormy past makes him the one man
Tess *doesn't* want protecting her....

Don't miss THE CASE OF THE MESMERIZING
BOSS by Diana Palmer, first in a lineup of
heroes MOST WANTED! In June, watch for THE
CASE OF THE CONFIRMED BACHELOR...only
from Silhouette Desire!

SDDP-1

MOST WANTED

YOU'VE ASKED FOR IT, YOU'VE GOT IT!

MAN OF THE MONTH: 1992

ONLY FROM
SILHOUETTE® *Desire*™

You just couldn't get enough of them, those sexy men from Silhouette Desire—twelve sinfully sexy, delightfully devilish heroes. Some will make you sweat, some will make you sigh . . . but every long, lean one of them will have you swooning. So here they are, men we couldn't resist bringing to you for one more year. . . .

A KNIGHT IN TARNISHED ARMOR
by Ann Major in January

THE BLACK SHEEP
by Laura Leone in February

THE CASE OF THE MESMERIZING BOSS
by Diana Palmer in March

DREAM MENDER
by Sherryl Woods in April

WHERE THERE IS LOVE
by Annette Broadrick in May

BEST MAN FOR THE JOB
by Dixie Browning in June

Don't let these men get away! *Man of the Month*, only in Silhouette Desire.

MOM92JJ-1R

Take 4 bestselling love stories FREE

Plus get a FREE surprise gift!

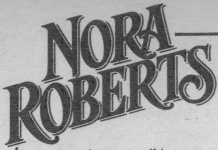

NORA ROBERTS

Love has a language all its own, and for centuries, flowers have symbolized love's finest expression. Discover the language of flowers—and love—in this romantic collection of 48 favorite books by bestselling author Nora Roberts.

Starting in February, two titles will be available each month at your favorite retail outlet.

In March, look for:

Irish Rose, **Volume #3**
Storm Warning, **Volume #4**

In April, look for:

First Impressions, **Volume #5**
Reflections, **Volume #6**

Collect all 48 titles and become fluent in

THE LANGUAGE of LOVE